THE
SPIRAL

Iain Ryan is an Australian writer who lives in Melbourne. He is the author of two previous novels, *Four Days* (2015) and *The Student* (2017), both of which were shortlisted for the Ned Kelly Award.

THE
SPIRAL

IAIN RYAN

ZAFFRE

First published in the UK in 2020
This edition published in 2021 by
ZAFFRE
An imprint of Bonnier Books UK
80–81 Wimpole St, London W1G 9RE
Owned by Bonnier Books
Sveavägen 56, Stockholm, Sweden

A CIP catalogue record for this book is
available from the British Library.

Paperback ISBN: 978-1-83877-141-6
Hardback ISBN: 978-1-83877-302-1
Trade paperback ISBN: 978-1-83877-303-8

Also available as an ebook and audiobook

1 3 5 7 9 10 8 6 4 2

Typeset by Palimpsest Book Production Ltd, Falkirk, Stirlingshire
Printed and bound in Great Britain by Clays Ltd, Elcograf S.p.A.

MIX
Paper from
responsible sources
FSC® C018072

Zaffre is an imprint of Bonnier Books UK
www.bonnierbooks.co.uk

To my sister, wherever she is

If you're trapped in the dream of the Other, you're fucked!
Gilles Deleuze

PART ONE

2004

ERMA

The plastic door jolts and a man shouts, *Come on.*

I open my eyes, wipe my mouth.

Another filthy airplane bathroom. Another mirror.

All this off the back of one email. It came through in Gijon, two minutes before my keynote. Subject line: *Disciplinary Action Pending. Dr Erma Bridges is advised*, and so on. *Meeting scheduled*. Rattled, I blasted through my presentation then sat in the corner of the conference dinner (dead-eyed, alone) before retreating to my hotel to pace around and call the travel agent. That's how I ended up on a thirty-four-hour flight back to Brisbane, back to the campus, back to confront this *meeting* head on, to show my face.

This face.

I hit the Centre by 8 a.m., coming straight in: plane cabin to customs to cab. The disciplinary meeting starts at nine. They aren't expecting me. That's why I'm here.

My office neighbour, Kanika, is already in for the day. She gives me the once-over. 'Have you showered?'

'Sure.'

'It doesn't look like it. Come here.' She takes a hairbrush from her drawer and hands it over.

'How's Harlowe?' Harlowe is my cat, a jet-black short-hair who set up house in my apartment two years ago. Despite his mysterious origin, Harlowe gets a bit fretful when I'm away. Kanika's between rentals, so she's cat-sitting.

'He's a fucking little turd,' she says. 'He's killing everything in your yard. You know that, right? Birds, lizards, mice. He even killed a snake. I didn't know we had snakes in New Farm.'

'Well, he's a cat.'

'They're not all like that.' She points at my head. 'Hair.'

I pull a clump of Kanika's thick mane from the brush and start pulling it through.

Kanika says, 'Are you worried about this meeting?'

'I came back from Spain for it, didn't I?'

'I don't know. Did you? No one's saying a word. HR set a separate meeting with me next week.'

'They ask you to bring anything?'

Kanika shakes her head. 'Just a meeting. Do you know what this is *actually* about?'

'Nope.'

'You sure, Erma?'

'It has to be about Jenny, right?'

'Fucking Jenny.'

And here it is: Jenny Wasserman, my research assistant, the problem child. Jenny and I had a falling out before I left for Spain. We ended up screaming at each other outside

4

a nightclub at four in the morning. It was bad. A big mistake. But for months now Jenny has been creating delays. She wants more money, *for transcription*, she says. *It takes forever.* It's a fucking shakedown, is what it is. I'm writing a book off the back of her work for me and she knows it. Her job was to conduct thirty interviews and transcribe the audio. Now, I have twenty-five interviews and an important missing piece: a face-to-face with Archibald Moder. The celebrated author. The recluse. No one gets to talk to him. But Jenny somehow got it done.

And now she's screwing me around.

'You want me to come in with you?' says Kanika.

'No.'

'I'll come in with you.' She spins in her chair. 'Can I ask how the book's going?'

'No, don't ask me that. How's this?' I nod at the wall beside us. This is Kanika's project. One whole side of her office is adorned with fourteen postcard-sized photographs, each with a name and date listed on a small sticker underneath. This is the result of a three-year research fellowship looking at representations of missing women in the Queensland media. The project's located here because the university has a history. We've lost fourteen female students in a decade. Three are dead. The remainder are at large. Some have been spotted. Some have called home once or twice. The majority are missing, presumed dead like the others. It is this sombre wall display that has earned Kanika's office its nickname, 'The Squadroom'. And it's true. Her

5

wall is like something out of a detective novel. Recently, it's become more and more like the dramatic end of that novel: Kanika drinks in here, eats in here, sleeps a couple of nights a week on a yoga mat on the floor. I'm no different. My work isn't as life-or-death, but I sleep in my office too. Thing is, I keep my office tidy and there are no pictures of dead girls on the wall, so no one calls my office anything.

At five to nine, a procession of admin people files past. The front three are dressed in formal greys and black but a straggler, a young man, is dressed like a student. He locks eyes with me. Seconds later, Kanika's desk phone rings. She answers it, puts the receiver down. 'Here we go then.'

My boss is Howard Chandler. His office is the kind of academic accommodation they don't make anymore: spacious, comfortable, quiet, three tall windows that catch the morning sun. Today, Howard is warming himself in that sun, sitting with his arse on a short filing cabinet. He doesn't look happy: he has his glasses off and he's furiously rubbing at them with a handkerchief. 'You shouldn't have come back for this,' he says, as a greeting. 'But now that you're here, take a seat over there.' He puts Kanika and I off to one side, against the wall. The people from the procession are clustered around a small round table Howard reserves for student consults. Howard turns to them and says, 'You better tell her who you are.'

The admin people introduce themselves. I try to memorise the names:

Delia Something, Deputy Director of HR.

Tall like a vampire.

Beside her is Donna, her assistant. Assistant to the deputy.

Redhead.

Then there's a man called Aaron Frill. He says he's the Assistant Dean but he can't be assistant to the Dean of Research because I've never seen him before.

Zip-up boots, grey slacks.

Last is Danny Hemult. He says he's from the union.

The student.

'I asked Danny to join us,' says Howard. 'What is this about? There's no agenda attached to the appointment and, to be bloody honest, I don't like coming in this early. It messes up my wife's schedule and that fucks up my schedule.'

'We've had a complaint,' says Delia.

'Complaints,' clarifies her assistant.

'Yes, that's right. Complaints.'

'And they pertain to?' says Howard.

'Misconduct.'

'Of a personal nature.'

Howard goes over to his L-shaped desk and sits there, apart from all of us. 'OK. What sort of misconduct are we talking about here?'

'We can't disclose the details,' Delia says. 'But we're going to need to speak with . . .'

Her assistant has a pile of loose-leaf pages on her lap. She lifts one and reads, 'Cynthia Dunstan.'

'Cynthia?' I hear myself whisper. She's a former postgrad of mine.

'Yes,' says the assistant. 'And David Brier. I believe he's a PhD candidate here. And then there's . . . one, two, three others, all postgrads who've been attached to the School at some point. Ryan Solis, Dylan Copson and Anita Milburn.'

No mention of Jenny.

Definitely the complainant, then. They can't name her.

They all turn and look at me. I don't know what I'm supposed to do. I say, 'Anita's not even—'

'No, I'm sorry but hold on, Erma,' says Danny Hemult. He's terrified. 'What is the exact nature of these complaints? Let's start there.'

I thought we had started there but Delia answers it. 'That's to be determined.' She stares into space as she says this, either completely unable to deal with conflict or flat-out dangerous.

Her assistant is a lot clearer. 'I *said* it was personal.'

Howard sighs. 'Have the police been contacted?'

There's a pause.

The assistant says, 'No.'

'Then get the hell out of my office. All of you.'

Delia turns quickly. 'We're here today to—'

'What? Get our permission to talk to these students? You don't need it, and if you did, then, no, you can't have it. Or do you want me to talk to them? Or to her?' Howard squeezes out a laugh. 'Find someone else to do your job for you. Or maybe, just talk to Erma yourself, ask her about what she's supposed to have done and go from there.'

'We can't do that,' says the assistant.

'She's right,' says Danny. 'They can't do that.'

I stand up. No control now. 'I'm right here.' I'm jet-lagged, scared, over-caffeinated. 'I'm right here! I'm not in Spain where I'm supposed to be, I'm not writing my book, I'm not in Singapore where I was nine hours ago. I'm right—'

'OK, Erma, OK, OK,' says Howard. 'What about you, Aaron? Do you have anything to add to all this?'

I'd almost forgotten about the Assistant Dean of Whatever. As Kanika hustles me towards the door, Aaron Frill draws back his lips and shakes his head. 'She's sleeping with her students.'

9

It's 9.48 a.m. The red vinyl punching bag in front of me compresses and re-forms, compresses and re-forms. I can hear the counter rhythm of my punches bouncing around the rest of the campus gym. There's only one person in here with me: a short Japanese woman working on ladder drills. She's way over the other side of the room but the sound of her feet slapping the mats blends into what I'm doing.

Jab.

Cross.

Jab.

Kick low.

Jab.

Low cross.

Jab.

Kick.

With the rage burning off, I lose count of the reps. My vision blurs. I push harder and the names float through the routine, consonants landing with each strike. *My victims*, apparently. I feel tears coming up. The floor tilts. Saliva foams in my mouth. I keep punching. I keep sweeping low with my leg.

Jab.

Cross.

Jab.

Before I have much of a handle on it, I find myself kneeling over the bin by the gymnasium mirrors hurling airline food into a plastic liner. It all happens to the pattering step-work of the woman behind me. To my eternal relief, she doesn't break from her workout. She doesn't ask if I'm OK.

Here's what's at stake. This is my academic career in a nutshell. Straight out of high school, I did a quick business degree in Melbourne, then fell out with my family and came north to my first office job in the Queensland state government. Hated it. So I started a coursework masters in arts. I graduated with a seven average, which led to research work for Griffith Uni, sessional tutoring for UQ, and, eventually, an APA scholarship and the research job I have now. In that research position, I'm full-time on my book, the one Jenny is stalling. The working title, *Secret Interactions: A History of Reader-Deployed Young Adult Fiction*. It's about the books of my childhood, the Choose Your Own Adventure novels, Fighting Fantasy gamebooks, Archibald Moder's Zone Mover series and the vast array of spin-offs and extensions these books introduced to YA fiction in the eighties. This topic was a surprisingly easy pitch to publishers. Those novels are full of cultural studies tropes: postmodern fracture, non-gendered protagonists – always presented in the second person *you* – and characters of ill-defined race, class and creed. I had multiple offers to publish. And it was more than just a good pitch for career advancement. It was personal.

I own a vast, vast collection of these novels. When I was a kid, my father brought them home from all over the world and I kept collecting them way past the age where the hobby seemed appropriate. I clearly remember reading them in the latter half of high school. Then later, my sister and I revisited them while I was home from uni, spending a long painful summer inside those branching narratives and arcane gaming systems as my family fell apart. At final count, my sister and I own over four hundred paperbacks in the genre, all carefully stored in the basement of the Centre.

I willingly levered this obsession of mine into my career. Working on something you love makes you productive. It's why academics spiral into workaholism. It's how I did it. I've put my whole life into *Secret Interactions*. And the rewards are coming, if I get the manuscript finished in the next month.

I'll be twenty-eight years old.

A full-time academic.

Research-only.

A regular keynote at conferences.

Writing a big book that people are waiting on.

And when I'm promoted – almost a lock, at this stage – I'll be the School's youngest associate professor. The youngest. So sure, it's been a rough couple of years – I've lost friends and family and I'm alone and notice it more and more – but I'm also getting exactly what I want. At an age when most people barely know their place in the world – while everyone's Saturn is in return ripping through their lives like a black curse – I'm getting over.

Or I was.

Until Jenny.

My muscles twitch. The gym shower blasts down and a cloud of grey steam envelops me. There's dark red blood snaking down my fingers.

David Brier.

Dylan Copson.

Anita Milburn.

Cynthia Dunstan.

Ryan Solis.

And Jenny.

No one said her name, but she was there.

The originator of all this. The architect.

Jenny the common denominator.

Jenny who knows all those people.

Jenny who binds them together.

Jenny and me.

Jenny was like a little sister to me, at the start. I saw myself in her. I encouraged her. Hired her. She's been to my apartment multiple times. I liked her for a lot of reasons but mainly because she wasn't a *sweet* woman. She didn't aim to please strangers. She appeared to have so much sly self-loathing in her that it made her unassailable, outspoken, interesting. She once told Howard – to his face – that one of his papers *sucked*, because why not. What could he say – or anyone else – that could be worse than what she told herself every day. But the flipside of that soon availed itself. Jenny just couldn't get out of her own way. Self-loathing is also self-obsession. Jenny got so petty and particular. So weirdly money hungry. She totally lost sight of our professional relationship. Kept making it personal. Kept assuming the work was secondary. That's exactly the vibe I *didn't* want from her. I wanted the self-critical, overcompensating Jenny. The brutally honest Jenny. But, over time, she became more and more like my actual sister, Dora, who trades in the same currencies of personal obligation and dependency. I don't have the bandwidth for any of that.

Thankfully, I'm not as close to the rest of the people on that list HR read out. I met the first one, David Brier, two years ago, at Ric's Bar after some work function. He had a white wine cask loose in his backpack and offered me a pour. Right there in the club he told me about his two failed passes at a PhD scholarship, then pitched me at 3 a.m. It worked. The second one, Dylan Copson, used to live with David in a share house three blocks from my place in New Farm. Dylan already had a PhD scholarship, and a girlfriend: Anita Milburn, who is supervised by Roberta Binyon, one of the poets on staff. David, Dylan and Anita all kicked around the School, then the Centre. They all did research assistant work for us. They all worked alongside Jenny. The last two, Cynthia and Ryan, are more like former colleagues. They were in the sessional teaching pool alongside Jenny a few years back but have moved on. I co-supervised Cynthia's PhD. I sat in on Ryan's thesis reviews. That's the extent of my scholarly involvement. When I met all these people, I was an overachieving twenty-five-year-old and they were early-twenties arts degree alumni scratching for scholarships and work. Until two hours ago, that's all it was. People who knew each other. People who worked together and lived near each other. It wasn't some corporate hierarchy. It's a university. We're all glorified students.

In the gym showers, I lift my busted knuckle to my mouth and taste coins and sea salt. My stomach rises, trying to push up through me again, but I breathe into it, slowing myself down. There's only bile left now. I can smell it.

I'm in trouble.

I know.

I should reach out to that union rep, the kid Howard invited to the meeting. *I should do that.* But I'm ashamed to admit that as a purveyor of critical theory and literary studies – two disciplines forged in Marxist critique – I'm not in the union.

I'm on my own.

I call everyone mentioned in the meeting and no one picks up. I send emails and get an immediate response from David Brier. He's on campus. He's procrastinating. He tells me he has a chapter due – which is news to me as his supervisor – but he agrees to a coffee without asking why.

I sit on the lawn by his office, in the afternoon shadows. I watch him schlep out of the Michie Building, tall but always slightly hunched over, as if too tall. His hair is kept short but it's never neat and the same could be said of his work uniform: brown corduroy trousers and an oversized knitted sweater. This is all part of his appeal. David hasn't grown into himself yet. He wouldn't look a bit different in his high school uniform.

'Aren't you cold?' he says, standing over me.

'What? This? I'm from Melbourne.'

'I need that coffee you promised me.'

'Merlo's closed. Have you seen Jenny?'

'No. Why?'

'She disappeared on me and she's been extra weird lately. Now she's causing trouble.'

'None of us in the postgrad room talk to her anymore.'
'Really?'

'The last time I saw Jenny, she was screaming at me from across the street in the Valley one night. It was fucked up,' he says.

'When was this?'

'Ages ago.'

'Last year?'

'More like the start of semester.'

'I thought you two were OK?' David and Jenny used to fool around.

'We were, well, sort of OK,' says David.

'So why was she yelling at you?'

'How the hell should I know? That's what she's like sometimes. What's this about?'

I stand up and dust the grass clippings from my hands. 'Has anyone from the uni contacted you recently?'

'About what?'

'About me. About . . .' And I wave my finger between the two of us.

David smirks, the little arsehole. 'About *us*? Bloody hell. What's going on?'

'Have you told anyone?'

'No.'

'You sure?' I know the answer. It's all over his face. He's insulted that I've lingered on this.

'No, Erma. I haven't told a soul. I promise.'

Boys like David Brier are always in my orbit for some

17

reason. Nice men who offend easily. All honour and valour over the little things. I flash back to David here insisting on accompanying me to the GP for the morning-after pill and the memory of it grinds.

I start backing up and say, 'I think Jenny's behind something going on with HR. If someone from admin comes and talks to you, say whatever you like, but just know that that's where it's coming from.'

'Erma, what? Wait.'

'Tell them whatever you like.'

'Wait. Wait.'

I hold up my hand in a muted wave for goodbye.

He says, 'Jenny said something about that.'

This stops me. 'About what?'

'On the street at the start of semester. She was screaming all sorts of crazy shit, but she mentioned you and me.'

'What did she say exactly?'

'She was acting crazy.'

'Just tell me.'

Nice guy David averts his eyes. 'Something like, "Go fuck that whore who got you into uni." Something like that.'

I feel myself wince. I take off, walking way too fast now. *Fucking Jenny.*

You little—

'Erma!'

Talk about cutting to the chase for once in her good-for-fucking-nothing life.

'Erma!'

If Jenny's out there, I'm going to find her.
You hear me, arsehole?
Tonight.

Jet lag is a miracle drug. I catch the bus into the city where I wolf down coffee and a cheeseburger then change buses and start searching through the Valley. This is Fortitude Valley but it's anything but. It's Brisbane's nightclub district, a place where pain and adversity are created rather than defied. I start at the bottom of the barrel tonight, which is RGs, The Royal George Hotel at the top of the mall. It's two-for-one jug night and it's already a nightmare. Clumps of students I recognise sit out in the beer garden, all keeping politely clear of the day drinkers and ranting junkies. A tense standoff.

A kid from my cultural studies reading group invites me to come sit with him. We drink room temperature VB while I scan around. A girl at our table mentions discount cocktails at The Empire. An older guy from a band comes past with flyers for The Shamrock. The warm beer churns in my gut.

No sign of Jenny.

I pour my dregs into a planter box and make to leave. As I stand up, the kid from the reading group says, 'I might see you later, yeah?'

'Sure. Where are you headed?'

'610. Then The Depot.'

This is a good start. There's a lot happening tonight and

I've already got a bad vibe. She'll be out. Jenny always prefers grit over glamour. She'll be here somewhere, darkening up some corner.

Outside RGs, I stand in the crowd streaming through the mall and check my phone for messages, thinking of my next move. Out of the corner of my eye, I see something smack into a guy's face. A plastic beer jug skids past my feet. The guy slowly slumps over. His friends gather round. Meanwhile, a scream belts out from back inside RGs. We all turn and watch as a stocky shirtless man stands on a wobbly table in the beer garden. He hurls another empty jug out at the crowd, followed with, 'Fuck my cock. Fuck my fat—' Security crash-tackle him to the ground and his body lands with an ugly wet thud.

As I was saying, this isn't the greatest part of the city.

Ric's Bar is empty. The cute guy (Rowan) playing records tonight is a friend of Jenny's so I hang out by the Galaga machine and sip water. Rowan sticks to his B material, careful not to blow his load over the post-work suits.

'Eye' by the Smashing Pumpkins.

Portishead live in New York.

'Spit on a Stranger'.

People come and go.

No Jenny.

10.15 p.m. I push on.

The Empire is empty. Two lesbians sipping Cosmos at the bar. A table of tourists.

The Zoo has a twenty-dollar cover charge.

At The Troubadour the band has already started and it's some terrible country-rock thing, and the room is full of beards and Nancy Sinatra knock-offs. These are not Jenny's people. The bartender there is a former student and he has the coffee machine on. I grab a long black, Irish style. Feeling momentarily invigorated, I hit 610, a dingy rehearsal studio and ad hoc venue up the street. Inside, I wade through the smoke machine fog and up the stairs to the small kitchen and it's there that I find Dylan Copson, already loaded, hitting on a short girl wearing what looks like a maid's costume from a sex shop. I plant myself beside him. Dylan glances over but doesn't say hello.

'I don't think any of this is true,' I announce loudly, interrupting him mid-sentence.

'Who are you?' says the girl in the costume.

'This is Erma. She's my . . .' Dylan screws up his face, reaching back through the haze of whatever he's on. 'You taught me "Intro to Media Studies", didn't you?'

'Among other things. Are you old enough to be in here?' I say to the girl. 610 is run by a teenager and they let anyone in.

'I'm nineteen.'

'Good for you. Can I borrow this idiot?'

I take Dylan's hand and drag him away before either of them can answer. There's a fire escape downstairs and I lead Dylan through it, out into the dark alleyway that runs

21

along the side of the building. The alley is suspiciously wet under foot and smells of bleach and cigarettes. Dylan's laughing. I don't know why.

'Have you seen Jenny?'

'What? Tonight?' he says.

'Yeah. Remember Jenny? Baby-faced, blonde hair, the girl you cheated on your girlfriend with. Ringing any bells?'

'What? That was you. I was with Jenny after that.'

This is true. And, for the record, while I did teach Dylan 'Introduction to Media Studies', nothing happened while he was in undergrad. Nothing. Our fling happened later.

'Dylan!'

He wipes his brow. 'Fuck, all right. Nah. I haven't seen Jenny in ages.'

'You sure?'

'Yeah, I'm sure. Jesus, why are you being so weird?'

I step closer so I can see his eyes. It's too aggressive. I sense it immediately.

Dylan breathes beer onto me. 'Can you just—'

'Jenny. Where is she? I know she's hiding from me.'

'I honestly haven't seen her. No one's seen her. Last time I saw her it was . . . it was for like ten seconds, on campus.'

'When was that?'

'I dunno. Back in April. Fuck, could have been even earlier, hey. It's been ages.'

'How do I find her? Where would she go if she's avoiding everyone?'

'I don't know.'

'Where is she living at the moment?'

'No idea.'

'None? Weren't you fucking dating her six months back?'

'I didn't date her. We just fooled around. I hooked up with Jenny after you, which was, like, two bad ideas in a row.'

I grab Dylan by the arm and drag him in real close, our faces an inch apart. 'I *am* a bad idea at the moment, Dylan. You hear me? And *you're* a fucking bitch. Stay away from that girl inside.'

He's so surprised it takes a moment for the anger to flare up. 'Let me go.'

'You better not be lying to me, Dylan. And you better not be talking shit about me behind my back.'

'Fuck, Erma, OK, OK.'

I let him loose.

We stand there a second. He rubs his arm.

'And you better be working on that lit review for Howard. I recommended your dumb arse for that gig, so don't make me look bad.'

'Jesus, OK. Why are you like this?' he whines. 'It's Friday night.'

'It's *Thursday* night, dickhead.'

I'm ashamed to say it but I've always been a little bit

mean to Dylan. A bit rough and prickly. Never quite like this but always sharp and impatient. He reminds me of someone I hate. This guy called Euan. They look the same.

I'm fading. I drag myself to The Depot and it's a nightmare, a total collision of flesh and booze. I have a gin and tonic. I do the rounds.

No Jenny.

At the edge of the dance floor with my face washed in orange swirling light, I start to wonder if I'm losing my mind a little bit.

Maybe it's not all about Jenny?

Maybe she's going to turn up with the transcripts tomorrow?

Maybe I should just pay her . . .

Maybe this is all me?

But no, that's not where it's headed. It's not where it started either. Not really. I tell myself, *We're just going to talk this out.* I'll find her tomorrow. Or the day after tomorrow. The orange light keeps coming, rolling over and over in sync with the music.

Where is my luggage?

At the office?

At the gym?

I was in a foreign country this morning.

I live on Moray Street, a long bowed road around the edge of New Farm, which is the suburb next to the Valley. I'm halfway there on foot when I realise there's one more place I need to check: the Alibi Room, my local.

I find Jenny's sister Gloria holding up the bar. Gloria's a little thinner than Jenny and a little taller but it's the same deal. They both have that ghostly hot-girl thing going on. Too weird to be beautiful but always threatening to grow into it. I take the stool beside her and pour us both a cup of water from the canister on the bar.

'Rough night, Glory?'

She lifts her head. Her eyeshadow's a mess. 'What the hell do you want?'

'I'm looking for your sister.'

Gloria's eyes blink and then, without a word, she starts gesturing around so wildly that I need to steady her on the stool. 'You know . . . Jenny's in sooooo much trouble. Sooooo much trouble. My parents are gonna . . . fucking . . . kill . . .'

'Where is she? Do you know?'

'Nobody knows, man! Nobody!'

The barman glances over. I push the water Gloria's way. She tilts her head sideways and lays a cheek flush against the bar. She looks at me through the glass, a giant fisheye watching.

'Am I OK?' she says.

'I think so.'

'I mean, I hope *she's* OK. She's missing. *Missing* missing. She was staying with me and with my folks, kinda splitting her time . . . but . . . my folks called the cops a week ago. No one's seen her, no one's seen her in . . . She's just fucking gone. Have you seen her? You must have seen her.'

I take a sip of my water. 'I've been away.'

The house music cross-fades from Idlewild to the Yeah Yeah Yeahs. The staff are watching us now. I figure Gloria's been a nuisance tonight.

Someone taps me on the shoulder.

Quick glance: a guy in glasses. A stranger.

'No,' I say.

He taps again and when I ignore it, he says, 'Glasses or no glasses?'

Gloria gives him the once-over. She lifts her head and her face is wet with Christ-knows-what from the bar. 'Do it again,' she slurs.

The guy tips the glasses off then on.

'Off,' Gloria says. 'You don't need to . . . hide all that.'

I turn around. The boy has short brown hair and is wearing that terrible combo of a collared shirt under a regular T-shirt. He's completely unremarkable bar the eyes. The eyes are a piercing bright blue.

I tell him, 'Hey, buddy, fuck off.'

Gloria shushes me and laughs a plastic laugh. 'What's your name?'

'I'm Drew. I bet you'd look good in these. I bet you're a glasses-on type of girl,' he says. 'They make everyone look smarter.' It takes me a second to realise he's directing all this at me.

'I'm already smart enough.'

'I figured. You dress a little bit like a nerd. I like nerds.'

Gloria laughs again.

I lean forward. 'Your bullshit doesn't work on me, mate. Go back to Dungeons & Dragons or—'

'I love D&D,' he says.

'Hey, Drew, I'm serious. Fuck off or I'm going to get someone to toss you out.'

Drew holds up his hands and mouths, *OK*. Just to be sure, I watch him walk back to his friends. There's no high-fiving. One of Drew's friends is watching us but there doesn't seem to be anything serious in it. Still, it's that time of night. I ask the barman to call Gloria a cab and then I walk her out to the street. When the cab arrives, I say, 'Jenny'll turn up,' even though I don't know if it's true.

'Who?'

'Your sister.'

Gloria huffs. 'You know, she's always been weird,' and Gloria trips a little as I ease her into the cab.

I take Moray Street the rest of the way home. I'm so tired I can feel myself stumbling. My mind is a loose list of worries and thoughts. I can't fight them off.

Glasses on.

My keys. Where are my fucking keys?

Kanika.

. . . that whore who got you into uni.

Cold. Should've worn a jumper.

Is it technically Friday? Was Dylan right?

Glasses off.

I find my house.

My bed.

I call out for Harlowe but he doesn't come.

As I slip into sleep, I hear my voice murmuring, semi-conscious, *you, you,* before I roll down into the dream void and that's when the barbarian comes alive.

SERO

1

Through the glare comes grey and tan, then the browns of dirt, the black of ash. Thick ochre blood on the walls. A cave arches overhead and a flat plane of rock – a smooth stone pedestal – lies beneath you, hard like a spear skewered down the length of your body. You find your way upright. A breeze leads the way out to the forest. You stand naked in the rain letting the downpour wash the mud from your skin. You feel nothing. Not the cool temperature, not the sting of exposure. You stretch your arms and legs and your muscles burn, pushing through a hard tightness. There are scars and black tattoos that flex and move on your skin. This is the body of someone who kills for a living. A barbarian.

2

On dusk, you smell smoke in the air and follow it to a small valley and an encampment. Four orcs sit around a campfire under a makeshift hut. Their skin is the mottled green of a toad and each of them wears ragged armour cobbled together from a dozen armies. Their voices carry despite the rain. It sounds like Haraustian. They're drunk. Too drunk for a scouting party and too drunk for hunting. These creatures are out here alone.

Orcs from the west have a high tolerance for wine, so it's night before one of them breaks off and wanders into the darkness. He smells of horse manure and sweat, and his piss sprays piping hot against your legs as you collide with him, taking him down. You have his sword before a word is said and you plunge it into him. It's sharp, like a needle.

The three remaining orcs fight for their lives but do not last long. The first loses his head as you come into camp. The second is stabbed through the heart as he draws his blade. Only the third manages to spar with you, but he's unsteady on his feet and loses. He stares at you as he dies and his eyes are black like horses' eyes. There is no pleasure in this carnage, only a sense of familiarity and calm.

As you wipe down the blade, you see that this is a strange weapon you have found. It's shorter than you'd like. Lighter, too. You stake it into the soft ground and collect the bodies. The orcs have very little of value:

A small bag of gold.

A vial of yellow liquid in a strange triangular tube.

A necklace of children's teeth.

A map drawn in charcoal.

You take three of the orc bodies and hang them from the trees by their garments. Then you take the remaining one, the one you took the necklace from, and you cut him open like a piece of livestock. In the firelight, you butcher the body for eating, your hands steady and knowing, as if directed by a trance.

ERMA

Movement by the door.

A black room.

Hotel.

Spain?

No.

My laundry basket, my chair, my mirror.

Brisbane.

It's several seconds before my bedroom appears through the murk. I'm home, but something is wrong. A sound. It's not in the street. It's in the living room. Or the kitchen.

'Harlowe?'

In response, I hear a murmur, a human sound. A sob or a deep, deep breath.

I jolt up and see the silhouette. Someone is in the room. 'What?'

Harsh white explodes out of the shadows, followed by the roar of thunder and the ripping of my bed sheets, the quilt, the plasterboard by my head. Something else is opened, something suddenly wet and—

Gun shots.

Fired at me.

I try to escape.

I roll off the bed. The floor rises up.

The gun keeps firing.

Flash.

Flash.

Flash.

I hold up my hand and it bursts open, dark blood spraying my face. I'm screaming, and the silhouette is on me, its thighs over my thighs, pinning me down as a heavy metal object is slammed into me, crumpling my arms and shoulders and glancing off the side of my head. I bring my hands up to block the blows but the blows keep coming. I flail around, trying to attack, but it doesn't work. Another blow comes in and my vision blurs.

I fade out.

The barbarian.

A spiral.

The end.

I come to.

The silhouette is kicking me.

The room smells like fireworks.

I hear the slotting of metal into metal. *Reloading.* The silhouette stands at my feet, a dripping gun in its hand. The gun comes up and it's aimed at me. I try to say no but nothing comes out.

The gun snaps. No light. No flash.

'Fuck me,' says the shadow.

I know the voice.

The shadow lifts the gun to its head and pulls on the trigger.

Snap.

Snap.

Snap.

Sn—

The room strobes and I see Jenny's blank white face and her empty eyes as the side of her head flies apart.

PART TWO

10 MONTHS LATER
PROVINCE OF KRABI, THAILAND

ERMA

Morning light flickers through the canopy and the brown mud under my feet is loose, the result of a dawn shower. In the distance, I can see a road. I can hear the ocean. I keep running till I hit the beach. I wade out into the lukewarm sea.

I'm in Thailand.

On my back, floating in the water. Cream-coloured clouds overhead.

Late June, 2005.

Beautiful.

Easy.

And the sum total of pure chaos.

There's a book in the Choose Your Own Adventure series where you have to cheat. It's called *Inside UFO 54-40*. You're abducted by aliens and find yourself aboard their ship. In the story, the choices you make bring about the usual array of fatalities and happy endings but woven throughout are mentions of a better place, a penultimate ending. There's a paradise planet called Ultima. Thing is, Ultima is hidden. To find it, the reader has to flick through the pages of *Inside UFO 54-40* and manually find the passage. When a reader opens the buried section (pp. 101–104), they're welcomed into Ultima by two characters wearing golden wreaths, one of whom says, 'No one can choose to visit Ultima. Nor can you get there by following directions.' And as such, you are rewarded for refuting the reality of the book, for breaking it.

I've been thinking about *Inside UFO 54-40* a lot these last couple of months in Thailand. It's the only part of my previous life I've let in. I feel a kinship for it now because I didn't navigate myself to this place. It's like I skipped ahead and landed here. I cheated death and found myself welcomed into a strange new paradise.

Except it's real.

I almost died.

That wasn't a dream.

Jenny shot me two times. The first bullet is what my doctors called a through-and-through: it entered my right shoulder just above the collarbone and passed out the other side without ripping up anything too important. The second hit my left hand. That was more serious. It broke three bones and shredded tendons. But, on the whole, a miracle. The worst and easily most embarrassing part of these injuries was the post-op infection in my shoulder from bullet number one. Apparently it pushed all sorts of garbage into my body as it moved through-and-through. No one knows exactly what the infecting material was, but the leading contender is bacteria-drenched fabric à la my clothes. I was sleeping in the shirt I'd worn that night to a half-dozen Fortitude Valley nightclubs. The two-for-one jugs of beer, the sweat and spit, the busted romances and bad breath, it all went into my bullet hole and almost killed me. That landed me in ICU for a week, which is a while, then ten days later I was back out in the world. At first, Kanika put me up in her new place just to help with my dressings. A month after that, I moved back to my apartment, to the empty answering machine and holes in the walls.

From there I went into months and months of physical therapy, hours of painful exercise and depressing training rooms and being around – or near, at least – people who had it far worse than I did. I was in rehabilitation with people missing limbs. These were people fucked up by auto accidents and war and industrial machinery. I was a tourist in their world. As one of my coaches, a former soldier, told me, 'You'll be fine. The person who tried to kill you obviously couldn't shoot.' My injuries were just a light sprinkling of near-death to those people.

And the part about Jenny's terrible shooting is certainly true. At the start, the police didn't tell me a lot, but I can count the bullet holes in my apartment. Jenny fired a six-shot revolver at me. No one could tell me how a postgrad with no experience with guns got this weapon but she did, somehow, and once she got hold of this exceptionally hard-to-find thing, she fired it at me until it was empty, then beat me with the gun so bad that the thing jammed with my own blood. The police detective in charge of the investigation told me I got lucky because – and here's the clincher – Jenny was *persistent*. The fact that she kept going until she eventually got the gun working again, that solved a lot of problems. I got lucky because Jenny is a lot better at shooting herself, it seems, than killing other people. Which is fine by me.

The Muay Thai training camp in Thailand was an idea I acted on quickly. The doctors and trainers cleared me to resume fighting in November – five months after the shooting – and having had a recent brush with death, I was keen to get back into it. At first, I used a gym near my house, going six days a week during the last gasp of 2004 and ignoring almost everything else.

My misdirections.

My stalled career.

My isolation.

My sister and my family and my research assistant Jenny who can't shoot and all the reasons why she might have—

Nope. Not yet.

Can't.

I took time off from my position at the university. They put me on some type of extended leave. Half salary. Negotiated end date. No pressure. I probably could have returned after three months. I was physically fit enough. But definitely not sane enough. I still sweated through the night, tossing and turning. I went days without long thoughts or conversation. Apart from the gym, I was a shut in. Didn't read a single email since the day I left work. My book contract, my research, the grant applications and acquittals and whatever else I'd promised people – reams and reams of promises – that was all up in the air. I was definitely between things.

There was no vacation responder.

No explanations to friends and family.

They didn't call anyway. Kanika was my emergency contact. The only living thing I had regular contact with was the cat.

I was a mess. Before the trip to Thailand, I cried every day, sometimes over exact memories, a lot of the time over nothing. I lived on steamed vegetables and cask wine. I read the fucking *Da Vinci Code*. As the Brisbane summer came on like nuclear fallout, I dragged a spare mattress into the living room and spent whole days and nights in there watching rented DVDs in front of the fan with Harlowe. When I could sleep, I dreamed of Sero the Barbarian, some abstraction from the Archibald Moder books I studied. The original novels are tales of journeys through foreign lands, heavy on bold quests, valiant action and dungeon running. My version was darker, more sombre, almost directionless. I think I dreamed weird stuff like that because I was barely living in the waking world.

I was alone.

The only time I felt good was in the gym.

I worked hard in there.

Low rep free weights with short breaks.

Body work. Resistance work. Cardio.

Endless drills for my right cross and low kick.

In the ring, I started to focus on attacking instead of defence. A long time ago, an old trainer of mine told me, 'This is Muay Thai. You're gonna get hit.' And pre-Jenny that's how I fought: in anticipation of getting hit. I blocked. I moved. I thought about my opponents strategically. I avoided getting hurt because I hated going to work with injuries. But that's all gone. Now I'm aggressive. I have long arms and yet I come in close.

I want to be near my opponent.

To feel her breath.

Blowing on me.

As I punch faceless stand-ins for Jenny.

Yesterday, in Thailand, my Krabi instructor Teng took our training session out into a grass field beside the camp. In the bright afternoon sunlight, Teng moved quickly, swinging into my side and neck with his rattan sticks, attacking me.

'You die. No head,' he said.

'OK. Again.'

I brought up my wooden swords. We fought. I ran my combination.

It didn't work.

'Again.'

Teng backed up. 'You know, the other guy told me you were getting good. But this . . .'

'Fuck off. Again.'

We went at it. I backed him up, got inside, tried for the femoral artery. But Teng is fast as shit and he found a way around. At the session's end, we rested in the grass. Me huffing and puffing. Teng hardly warmed up.

'You going home soon?' he said.

I nodded. I had extended my stay twice already. Extending it a third time felt wrong, like I might never go back.

Teng said, 'You want to date me? Last night tonight. Last chance.'

'No.'

'Why not?'

Teng has a look I can come at. Big around the arms. Brown eyes. But I wasn't tempted. Hadn't been in quite a while. Not since Jenny. 'Do you know why I came over here?'

He shrugged.

'Someone tried to kill me, back home.'

'You fight back?'

'I tried.'

'You win?'

'I guess.'

'Did you fuck him up?'

'It was a woman. And yeah, she's dead.'

Teng smiled at that. 'Maybe no date then. You're too dangerous for me.'

I drew a finger across my neck.

The lukewarm dusk sea.

On my back, floating.

The salmon-pink sky arcing overhead.

Late June, 2005, Thailand.

I close my eyes and let the water move me to and fro. I imagine myself from above, as if filmed through a camera from a satellite. I'm only here, in this place, this water, this beach, these exact geographic coordinates, because this is the path of my life thus far.

No lessons.

No answers.

It just happened.

I skipped ahead.

But today something stirs in me, something in the deep ocean below. In my mind, I sink down. I swim into the cold water. The light fades. I go into the dark excess. My eyes adjust. There's a black canyon on the sea floor and inside it I see something.

Two sickly white eyes in the shadows.

Brown-green tentacles silently floating.

I reach out.

Back home. Day One.

Brisbane in winter. Still bright as hell outside.

11.35 a.m.

It feels like a mistake.

The place sounds the same. Traffic on the street. Lawnmowers. Renovation. There's a pile of mail on the coffee table. My luggage still in the hallway from last night.

I go to the answering machine and press the button.

You have three missed calls.

The first missed call is from . . .

Some telemarketer.

I hit the button.

Next message: *Hello, Miss Bridges?* A man. *Hello?* The man coughs twice, and the line goes dead.

I hit the button.

The third call is from . . .

My mother's voice fills the room. 'Hello, dear. We're selling the house. I wanted to call and say that. I'm sick of cleaning the damned pool, if you must know. So, if

45

you want any of your old things, maybe you should arrange to have them shipped up to wherever the hell it is you're living at the moment. Your father . . . your father—'

I hit delete.

I head straight to the gym.

On Day Two, Kanika visits without invitation. We stand in the little courtyard at the front of my place and drink stove-top coffee. She looks me over and says, 'You look thin.'

'Thanks.'

'It wasn't a compliment.' Kanika grabs my arm and lifts it up, as one might handle a pet. 'Strong though.'

'Sword work. I learned how to fight with one.'

'Every little girl's fantasy,' says Kanika.

'What's been happening here? How's Howard?'

'He's making noises about retiring, louder noises. But, aside from that, the Centre is still the same.' Kanika takes a cigarette from her purse and lights it. 'You meet anyone on your trip?'

'You mean, a guy?' I shake my head.

'You OK?'

'Better. I don't know where to start exactly but I'm thinking about work again.'

'Really?'

'What else am I going to do? Work in a 7-Eleven? I feel like I need to just . . . I don't know.'

'Well, I've got something for you, then.' Kanika tucks her smoke into the corner of her mouth and leads me out to the car. She opens the boot and stands back. 'There you go.'

A cardboard packing crate.

'Go on,' she says.

I hoist it out.

Two months ago, Kanika signed for a package at the Centre. A brown box. The sender: *Gloria Wasserman*. Jenny's sister.

When I'm alone, I open the box and carefully place the items on the kitchen table:

Three black Moleskine notebooks filled with Jenny's handwriting.

A thick pile of printed journal articles.

Two A3 mind maps in biro.

A plastic wallet filled with receipts.

Two overdue library books.

Four USB sticks.

A UQ-inscribed laptop charger.

A pencil case.

And more books. A dozen dog-eared textbooks filled with marginalia. My research copies of *Forest of Doom* and *Secret of the Ninja*. A vintage copy of *Inside UFO 54-40*, the Ultima passage marked with a Post-it. She also has *Zone Mover 29: Dark Corridor* by A. S. Moder, the distinctive series logo on the cover: an ornate shield locked inside a cube-shaped spiral. It's in bad condition. I scan through. *Dark Corridor* looks like all the books in the series. It's a branching narrative with numbered sections and line illustrations, the same elaborate ink-work by Elizabeth Goodman. The story revolves around a young family terrorised by an evil red-headed daughter who wears exaggerated black-rim glasses and has telekinetic powers. I put the book back and arrange Jenny's things in a tight grid on the table.

There's something off about this.

I stand on a chair, for a different angle. From above, I can see it all at once.

Research materials.

A project underway.

But too neat. Too orderly.

Organised, even. Too organised for . . .

Jenny wasn't flaking out.

Jenny was working.

I go cold. Jenny didn't seem human that night in my room. But here, on my kitchen table, there is proof of her humanity, her complete lack of psychosis. I stay up on the chair and stare into her stuff. It takes a while but finally another thought arrives.

I say it out loud, 'Where's the interview, Jenny?'

The irreplaceable interview with Moder, the once-in-a-lifetime opportunity.

All that pain and suffering for naught without it.

★

My kitchen walls are painted an orange-cream colour. Above my kitchen bench there's a long space I've filled with posters and clutter. I tear it all down and wipe the paint with a washcloth then dry it with a tea towel. I take a set of Jenny's pencils and draw a line. About a third of the way along, I write her name, and underneath I mark a date.

'July, 2004'.

That's the night she tried to shoot me. But I hired her in the winter of her first-year post-thesis, so there's a lot of space before July. I back up and look at this timeline with one marking on it. I look at the blank spaces, either side. Somewhere on this line, there are answers.

I go back to her stuff on my kitchen table.

I look through her USB sticks.

I open her work journals.

I log receipts.

I transcribe everything onto the line.

For the first time in months, I feel like my old self. It actually feels good to work. Research is research, I guess, In my bed that night, as I dream of the timeline, my mind starts to work through the details, the connections. The cross-fade between my new project and the epic fantasy of my barbarian dream proves seamless: I'm in the kitchen, scratching at the wall with a pencil, mapping data, then I'm following the timeline back – like a rope – into a sinister forest of drooling creatures and howling wind. In that dark wild place, I become a different person and I live inside that person. The barbarian. I see things I cannot see elsewhere. For example, I can see, with calm poise, that I am lost along every dimension. And yet, I keep moving forward.

SERO

3

Two days pass in the forest but the rain and the canopy render day as night and the journey is long and directionless. On the third day, the treeline breaks to a valley and down in the valley there is a small village dug into the earth, chimneys expelling smoke into the morning mist.

4

The streets of the village are empty, but you feel eyes on you. At the centre, there is a small store. A man stands in the doorway holding a rusted steel mace. He's short but has the proportions of a man.

'Halt there,' he says.

'I'm not here for thieving. I need a druid.'

'I see. What troubles you then?'

'I'm without memory.' It's true. You remember nothing before the cave from which you emerged.

The shopkeeper weighs the mace in his hand. 'What do you want with memories?'

You cannot answer this.

'Well?' he says.

'I should have them, shouldn't I?'

He shrugs. 'Sister Rhys can perform medicine. Do you have gold?'

'I have gold and I can work.'

The shopkeeper thinks on this. 'Yes, you look like the sort who can. Stand back a little. Move back to that stone.'

You do not understand the request, but you comply. The shopkeeper nods to himself then closes his eyes, as if in prayer. He begins to hum. His humming grows louder and the regular sound of the village fades away. Birds fly silently. Water drips into a well without note.

A door opens behind you, breaking the spell.

Footsteps.

'I'd stay put if I were you,' whispers the storekeeper, at a distance but uncannily loud in your ear.

A woman's voice says, 'This better be important, Brother Dal. I don't like to be disturbed this time of morning, not for the . . .'

The shopkeeper opens his eyes. 'Sister Rhys?'

'This one's marked with the spiral,' she says. 'All over its back.'

5

Sister Rhys has a wife who prepares food and a bucket of warm water. They have a spare bed for you but both the room and the lodgings are too small to accommodate your bulk, so they lay linens on the floor by the fire and you take to it and sleep despite the unknown dangers these people present.

The sleep is deep but broken by feverish dreams.

Dreams of war.

Blood dripping into an ocean.

Salt and sand whipping wind.

Red fire.

Black slugs.

A mouth torn open.

In the evening, the wife presents you with more food, this time accompanied by ale. As you eat and drink on the floor, you check your belongings:

Gold.

The sword.

A charcoal map.

A yellow triangular vial.

'Do you know what that contains?' says Rhys. She sits at the table, a book open in front of her.

'I took it from orcs.'

The two women exchange a glance.

'They're dead now,' you say. 'What is it?'

'May I?' Rhys takes the vial. She lowers her reading glasses and checks the liquid in the candlelight. Frowning, she takes a small sniff. 'Hmmm. I wouldn't drink this. Not out in the open.'

'What country are we in?'

'Emery, on the edge of Swann. So, it's true then? You remember nothing?'

'Do you know me?'

'Of course. Well, not you in particular but your kind. Your people helped clear this land. That spiral on your back, the ink there, that's a sigil familiar to the likes of me. Very familiar.'

'What does it mean?'

'Everything,' she says. 'Everything.'

'So, will you help me?'

'Our medicine won't work on you but I can show you a place on that map of yours where tall magic is performed. There is one there called Rohank.'

The wife pauses by the stove. 'You can't send him to the priest.'

'What choice do I have?'

'Some are the kind that ought not remember,' says the wife. She turns to you and adds, 'Have you thought of that?'

'I want to know.'

'Of course, you do,' says Rhys. 'But she's right. That thing on your back isn't about what you want. It's about what will be. About what's coming.'

'So, what is it then?'

'How would I know?' says Rhys. 'It's your tattoo. Not mine.'

ERMA

I finish mapping out Jenny's box of research materials on a bright Tuesday morning. I mark the details up on the wall and put a context around every date, time, place and person. My kitchen is filled now with biographical information, networks, academic milestones, personal memories, photos (where I had them) and locations and times.

Qualitative research 101.

The timeline is busy in the first half of 2004. April, May, June are a dense circuit of specifics: receipts for petrol, cafes and booze, notes from meetings, signed consent forms, schedules and field notes. I have data now, new connections. I know Jenny preferred pen and paper. I know Jenny drove everywhere and never took public transport. I know she stayed up late. Every interview or appointment happened after midday. She ate out and drank with interviewees.

I suspect she interviewed Archibald Moder while I was in Spain, which is a lot later than arranged.

So she lied to me.

Lied continuously.

Lied and crammed, condensing eighty per cent of a year's work into the three months before her death.

Two things are definitely missing:

Her car.

Her dictaphone.

The car is everywhere in the fieldwork. It's worth tracking down. So is the dictaphone. I'm fairly certain it contains her last five interviews. The interviews happened. They were consented to and the paperwork is here, but there are no copies of the audio. I take the paperwork for the Archibald Moder interview to the window and hold it up to the morning sun. Looks like she mailed it to him with a return envelope. Normally you get the interviewee to sign-off in person but for some reason they did it all in advance. I zoom in on Moder's handwriting on the form. It's the scrawl of an old man. Shaky. Uneven. But definitely the scrawl of my signed books, purchased from resellers on eBay. I've never met Moder in person. He hasn't appeared in public this century. He used to be a licensed psychotherapist and the word is that in his retire-ment he views interviews as work, even on the phone. He doesn't talk to anyone. And yet he spoke to Jenny.

My mobile buzzes. Kanika's number.

'Finally,' she says, as a greeting.

'I've been digging around in that box you gave me.'

'Of course you have. And?'

'Do you think the publisher would still be interested in my book?'

'Yes. They're an academic publisher, they're used to delays. How are you feeling, otherwise?'

'Good. Better. I feel better.'

There's a pause.

'I'm fine, by the way,' says Kanika. 'Thanks for asking.'

'You're always fine.'

'No, I'm not.'

I stare at the timeline.

Neither of us speak.

That Dictaphone is out there somewhere.

In a cafe.

A desk drawer.

A locker.

Police storage.

The glovebox of a car. Her missing car. Sessionals live in their cars. We call them highway academics for a reason. So that's the obvious place for it. *Not a great place for it, Jenny, but something fell apart at the end didn't it, some—*

'I'm late for something,' says Kanika.

The line goes dead.

'The Dictaphone and the car,' I say to the kitchen wall, the phone still pressed to my ear. 'And the police. The police will have some of her stuff.'

Harlowe meows at my feet.

I have the business card of one of the detectives who investigated my assault. It's in the drawer by my bed.

Find the Dictaphone.

Call the cops.

Find the car.

Three action items.

57

Three neat moves.

The timeline condensed.

That's what it tells me.

A starting point.

And, like a lot of research, it's an elaborate redressing for a one-word question: *Why?* But that's also the great thing about research. The process of it – the methodology, the collection, the analysis, the objectivity – it can bury anything.

I drive across town and park in the backstreets of St Lucia, then follow the river into campus, realising as I go that it's another winter at the University of Queensland. The teaching semester is over. Almost a whole year since Jenny.

There's a tech counter in the Social Sciences and Humanities library where postgrads borrow equipment. If Jenny got her Dictaphone from there, she may have returned it. I might be looking for a tape, not a device. Today, a tall kid in a baby-blue Shins T-shirt stands behind the counter, slowly winding up a black cable.

'You open?'

'Sure.' He stops winding but doesn't really move or look at me. His name tag reads, 'Bernard'.

'Bernie, I'm a staff member up in the CWCU. I think one of my postgrads returned a Dictaphone without wiping it.'

'What's the CWCU?'

'The Centre for Creative Writing and Cultural Understanding.'

'Never heard of it.'

'It's upstairs in Forgan Smith Tower.'

'We . . . we have a *tower*?'

I lean over the counter. 'Are you OK, Bernie?'

'I just didn't know we had a tower.'

'Her name is Jennifer Wasserman.'

Bernie ties off the lead. 'Try the book.'

I scan the entries of the logbook on the counter, searching for staff numbers from this time last year.

April 25th – Sanyo ICR – Wasserman.

Her signature beside it.

'This is her. Is this Dictaphone in here?'

Bernie wanders over to a shelf of equipment and looks around. 'It's gone. Your friend should bring that back or, oh man, she's totally gonna get banned forever.'

'She's dead, Bernie. So, she kind of is banned forever.'

'That's heavy.'

'Yeah. What does one of these things look like?'

He brings a Sanyo ICR over. It's a small silver device about the length of a glasses case, the sort of thing you could slip into a handbag or jacket pocket. Easy to lose.

'Bernie, if someone misplaced one of these, would it come back here?'

He turns the recorder over in his hands and shows me a sticker with the university's contact details on it. Below the sticker there's a number engraved on the surface. 'You can't hock them. Cashies call us straightaway. But they don't turn up all that often either, not when they're lost. Security might be able to help.'

'Really?'

'They look after the lost property locker.'

'Don't they go through it and return your stuff?'

'Nah. They don't like us, hey.'

'Do you ever go over there and check?'

'Nah. It's just me down here. What if someone needed something and I wasn't here?' He pauses. I can see now that Bernie's quite stoned. His hand is gently patting the Dictaphone like it's a small pet. 'Uhm, how did your student die?' he says.

'Shot herself.'

'With a gun?'

I nod.

'Bummer.'

'Not really. She was an arsehole.' It feels good to say it, even just to Bernie, but, moments later, I start to feel queasy. *Why did I just say that?* I think I'm going to cry, right there at the library AV counter. Heat washes down my neck.

Nope. Not yet.

Can't.

Oh fuck.

Look the thing is—

OK, the thing with Jenny is, there's no pinning down how to feel about her. That's why I don't open up that part of my brain. I mean, what choice do I have? If I am to remember her, what version of her is the right one? What role can I assign? What story? Is she my would-be murderer? My crazy ex-colleague? My dead friend? And

61

those are the simple stories, the easy designations. What do I do with the days before Thailand where I grieved for Jenny as a victim *and* hated her as her own murderer? Into what part of my mind can I pour the shame of my survival, the stifling lack of closure, the infinity of unsaid explanations? All of the ten thousand *whys* of Jenny Wasserman? Where do I put all of *that*? And it's not like there's a smooth transition between any of these different moods or representations. Not at all. She's not *contained*. All the ideas I have about her flicker inside me, rendering my life invisible in the blur. I'm done with feeling any of that. I'm done with Jenny and her—

No.

Just done.

Enough.

The swelling inside me resides, just in time.

I regain my breath.

Bernie is staring at me, seeing all this play out.

'It's complicated,' I tell him.

'Yeah,' he says. 'Yeah right.'

It starts to rain as I cross the campus to security. Inside the office, two uniformed guards claim to know very little about a lost-and-found depository but I cajole one of them into phoning someone else and together they direct me to a basement on the edge of the university grounds. It takes a while but eventually I find it. Down there, a security guard with a sandy moustache and a permanent squint tells me he can't let me inside to snoop around. Instead, he steps inside the depository on my behalf and returns with a plastic tray of dictaphones. There are dozens of them.

I sort through each one, looking for the make and model Jenny used. 'Jesus. What else do you have in there?'

'You name it, it's in there. When did you lose this thing of yours?'

'I didn't lose it. A student of mine did. Jennifer Wasserman. Would have been last year.'

He just shrugs as if to say, *Good fucking luck.*

I separate out the five dictaphones with UQ engravings on them. I run the numbers but Jenny's dictaphone isn't there. They're all empty. No tapes. 'You should return these to the tech office in the library. I reckon they're looking for them.'

'Sure,' says the guard. He sweeps them back into the tray with one fast movement. 'I'll get right on it.'

'Thanks for your help.'

At the foot of the stairs, I pause to listen to the rain falling outside. Winter rain is rare in Brisbane. 'Gonna be with us for a day or two, apparently,' says the guard.

'I don't suppose you have a spare umbrella in there?'

He shakes his head. 'Had to stop collecting them. It got to be that we couldn't close the bloody door.'

I had vague plans of dropping into the Centre to see Howard and Kanika and my office but I use the rain as an excuse to ditch. It's a mistake because after I cut through the Michie Building, I hear someone say, 'Erma? Is that you?' I'm halfway down the Michie's rear stairs, dripping wet. I shield my eyes and look. Anita Milburn stands under the alcove above, cigarette in hand. She does not look good. Anita usually has a fresh, wholesome quality to her – plaited ginger hair, lots of polos and sweaters – but today she's in a loose cardigan and has bags under her eyes. 'Holy shit,' she says.

'I've got to go.'

'I thought they fired you.'

I take off.

'They should have,' she shouts after me.

I don't know why but I actually wave to her, as if she's just said something completely different.

The windscreen fogs up in my car. I'm in the UQ car park, waiting out the rain. The lot is three-quarters empty this time of year and sitting out here alone doesn't feel right. The car is a cage around me. Something is creeping out from the edges of my mind, loosened up by this visit.

Something missing.

Or something found.

I close my eyes.

I move ideas around.

I hate it but I chart out another timeline and in my mind the line snakes across campus and through people I know, through Anita Milburn and her wretched face and fuck-you tone.

Anita is somewhere in the middle of that line.

I thought they fired—

Before all this, I had a boyfriend for a time. Two years, maybe two and a half. His name was Louis. We lived together while we both did the last stretch of our PhDs. I think that's what the relationship was about, our projects. A PhD can be lonely and we kept each other company.

That's all it was: a pooling of resources. A year after graduation Louis took a job in Chicago and a month into his new job he emailed to say he'd found someone new, a senior lecturer in cultural sociology at Northwestern. His new girlfriend was already a name. She's a full professor now. I'm sure they live in a nice place free of bullet holes.

I rebounded from Louis into Ryan Solis, a postgrad assigned to the Centre. Ryan looked a bit like Louis. He was also a year from wrapping up his thesis, so something was definitely going on. But Ryan wasn't much of an intellectual. I didn't see a lot of potential in him on that front. I wasn't his supervisor. I don't know why they named Ryan in the disciplinary complaint because all I did was sit in on his thesis presentations.

I read his work.

I gave him notes.

I signed his paperwork.

So, I guess there is some duty of care but . . .

Jenny introduced us. The whole thing didn't last long. A month or two. Ryan loved to drink and took to it like a first-year undergrad, even though he was twenty-three. I just couldn't be bothered with the endless socialising. The long nights in the Valley did nothing for me. I have no idea why our inevitable break-up hit him so hard. Ryan was good with women. He came from a good family. He was never going to fail at life, not entirely. And he didn't, he's a casual lecturer at Griffith these days. But when I dumped him, he apparently drank for a month non-stop and talked about suicide. Rumour was, he actually tried it. Jenny told me all this in a cafe in Paddington after she demanded we meet. She shared a house with Ryan and three other students, including Cynthia Dunstan, also on the list.

'Ryan's devastated,' Jenny said. 'Absolutely devastated.'

I'd seen her looking at Ryan. The *way* she looked at him after a few drinks. 'Why don't you fuck him then?' I said, standing up. 'Maybe that can be your job now.'

I don't know why she didn't.

Maybe she did?

Jenny was always cagey about boys.

Anita Milburn was next. Or I should say her boyfriend, Dylan Copson, was next. That was nothing. At the time, Dylan was a twenty-four-year-old postgraduate student, building up to a PhD bid with research assistant work. We did one contract together. One contract. It was a three-week job and for the last fortnight of it we fooled around. When the job was finished, Dylan turned in his report and I read it in my underwear in his bed.

It wasn't bad.

And that was Dylan in a nutshell: not bad.

But obviously not good either. He was stringing Anita along, not that I knew it at the time. That red hair of hers was everywhere in the apartment.

I just never asked.

I didn't really care.

Anita wasn't my student.

When Dylan was done fucking me on the side, he moved on to Jenny. There she is again, I suppose. It's weird, I can remember her telling me she liked him. In a way, I totally gave her her moment.

The rain falls hard and thick and I start to worry about hail. I wipe at the inside of the windscreen, searching the landscape for something to park my car under.

The lot is open.

There's nothing.

I thought they—

And then there's David Brier. I think David also got over on his physical similarity to Louis, the one who left me for the senior lecturer in Chicago who is now a professor. I'm the secondary supervisor on his thesis. Or was. Who knows? I quite like David but our time together was super brief. Four one-nighters, spread months apart.

That's it.

Of all these men, he's the only one I feel a twinge of *something* over. Not affection. It's not guilt. But whatever it is – proprietary, maybe? – I try to keep a purposeful social distance from him these days. It's nonsense, in a way. Overprotective on my part because David Brier can handle himself. He's painfully smart. And he's a Deleuze reader. Fucking his secondary supervisor a couple of times, it isn't nearly the dumbest thing he'll do in his academic career.

★

The rain blasts down and there's some new perspective in all this brooding. I suddenly sense Jenny's presence more keenly. She knew these men. She slept with Dylan, maybe slept with Ryan. She was on and off with David, like myself. That's student life, all over. If the postgrads didn't sleep with one another, none of them would ever get laid. *None* of them. But I don't like the triangulations forming. Jenny and I seem a bit joined at the hip. Stick sisters, through and through. And yet I was working with her, putting a lot of trust in her. Depending on this psycho for things I really needed. It seems kind of crazy now.

I thought—

I crawl into the back seat and lie down.

I flip the bird at the car ceiling and say, 'Fire this, bitch.'

I shut my eyes.

Maybe they should have fired me?

Oh god.

I haven't slept in a day or two.

Did I mention that?

SERO

6

You stagger out of the forest, covered in blood and dirt. You come across a wide lake of turquoise water. You scan the lake and see a house on the opposing shore. A small stone cottage.

7

There's a dead horse behind the stone cottage. Inside the house you find a thin man in battle armour tending to a fireplace. He kneels before the flames, eyes averted. You step in behind him.

'I have no gold and no food,' he says without turning. 'So be on your way, traveller.'

'What is this place?'

'None of your concern. I'm to start this fire or we'll both find ourselves at the end of a rope tonight.'

'I think not.'

The man sighs. 'The man coming this way has killed a dozen of your kind.'

'My kind? I'm unknown even to myself.'

'You have no name?'

'None that I can remember. I woke in a cave, in the forest.'

'You should go back there. Now, I best be—'

You draw your sword.

'Oh, I see,' and the man turns to you at last. In the firelight, his face appears ruined, a mess of open scars and wet blisters. 'Go on then,' he says. He unstraps his chest plate and it drops to the floor. 'You'd only be doing that which I haven't the courage for.'

'So be it.'

The man collapses fast when struck. For reasons unknown, you help him to the ground. Huffing his last breaths, the man smiles and tells you it's a pity not to see his masters die tonight.

8

The night is clear. Dressed in the dead man's clothes, you stand by the house and watch a party of riders approach. There are five of them. Two strong guards with armour catching the moonlight. Three without. Noblemen.

You return to the house and wait.

They arrive and tie their horses. One of them yells, 'Tyson? Where are you, goddamnit?'

The door slams open and one of the guards comes in alone. You step out from the shadows and slip an arm around his throat. He struggles terribly, his armour creaking and grinding against you. When it's done, you search his body and find a knife.

71

You leave through a rear door and circle the cottage. As you appear from the side of the house, you howl like a demon and throw the knife into one of the noblemen before plunging your sword into another. Blood splatters across your face and it feels like rain after years of drought.

9

You have a horse now. And you have gold. More gold. The noblemen were carrying bags of the stuff. You also have a week's supply of food and a range of weapons. The men carried daggers, maces, axes and swords. You look through the swords and test them but none of them feel right. You keep the strange blade you took from the orcs. There is one final item, though. The party of noblemen carried a hessian bag of severed hands. Trophies. You spread the hands out on the ground.

Fourteen men.

Five women.

This means nothing to you but a cold sensation washes through your body. You stare at your own hands, then you gather up the body parts and place them back in the bag as a harsh storm blows in, extinguishing the pyre.

ERMA

I come to gasping for air in the back seat of my car.

Night outside.

I've been asleep for hours in the UQ car park.

I get out and stretch my legs on the wet bitumen. Nearby, a street gutter roars with current. Drizzling rain falls through the street light.

Part of the barbarian dream still floats around in my head. I want to grasp hold of it – *the man with the damaged face, the hands in a bag* – but as I search the details, they seem to evaporate. *What is this?* Sero is Archibald Moder's creation. The character has been in my head since I was a teenager, but not like this. The dreams are a persistent thing now, post-Jenny.

I turn my face skyward and let the misting rain wet my skin, trying to wake up. Standing there in the dark empty car park, I feel strangely revitalised.

A weird idea arrives:

Reschedule with Moder.

Tell him what happened.

I have his number. It's in Jenny's paperwork. I could call him.

Why haven't you done this?
Reschedule the interview and you don't need Jenny's dictaphone.
Hedge a bet each way.

If I call Moder's people and tell them the whole story, he might bite, because he's a writer. Whatever his proclivities towards seclusion and privacy, the story of the dead girl he just met might pique his interest. Death and violence are always a great pitch.

Breakfast is a toasted sandwich at an espresso bar Jenny favoured, a hole in the wall down on James Street. It's on my timeline. Sitting on a milk crate in the winter breeze, I run my list from the other day:

1. *Find the Dictaphone.*
   —*Call the cops.*
   —*Find the car.*
2. *Reschedule Moder.*

I make the calls first but get no answer from the detectives in charge of Jenny's case or from Moder's people. I leave messages with both. Then I chart a course for the day, pen in hand, street directory at my feet. My next tasks – find the dictaphone, find Jenny's car – they're spatial now. Lost coordinates on a plane. Certeau said that we make and remake the city by walking through it, embodying it as if we're blood flowing through veins. Today, I'm Jenny's blood.

From my timeline, I know that Jenny goes dark in mid- to late June. Leading up to that I've got receipts and research notes that show her drinking eleven thirty double-shots here at Jamie's Espresso, eating late-afternoon burritos at Tuckeria on Brunswick Street and all-day breakfasts at Cirque. Some days she's working across the river in West End and over there it's coffee at The Gun Shop, yiros at The Little Greek, cocktails at the Lychee Lounge. She's a creature of habit. The same cafes and pubs depending on what side of town she's working.

My thinking is, she lost the dictaphone. Misplaced it. That's why she was stalling. That's the theory. The last interviews look like they happened. I have her schedule and the receipts. I can see her getting out there, doing them. The only interview I can't see concrete proof of is the one with Archibald Moder. All I have is the prelim paperwork on that. I don't have fuel receipts for driving out to his place up on Tambourine Mountain or food-stops dotting the journey but I'm still holding out hope. That interview was booked and arranged. All she needed to do was turn up with the dictaphone and the survey questions. Who knows? Maybe she didn't need food or fuel that day?

What I need to do now is a little fieldwork. I need to shake something loose. I'm going to visit all the places on her timeline and see what happens. This is the nature of all field research. New knowledge comes to those who show up.

Walking to the cash register, I notice a lull in the morning foot traffic. I order another flat white at the counter and, like some police detective in a movie, I hand over a picture of Jenny while they're making it. I found this picture tucked into one of her textbooks. It's the smiling Jenny, taken in New Farm park, rose bushes in the background. This is the living person. The young woman I knew. I've found I can't look at it for too long, not this particular photo.

'Do you remember this girl?'

The blonde woman on the register has better things to do. She glances at the photo and passes it to the man working the coffee machine. He shakes his head and hands the photo back.

'She was a regular,' says the man. 'Not in a while, though.'

'This girl had something of mine. A dictaphone. It's silver, the size of a mobile phone. Do you have somewhere you put stuff that's been left here?'

'When did she leave it?' says the man.

'A year ago.'

'It'd be long gone if it was ever here,' he says and puts my coffee up on the counter.

I receive a similar story from a dozen other cafes, pubs and bars. The Brunswick Hotel lets me sort through their disgusting bucket of lost things. It's all in there: Zippo lighters covered in grease, frayed paperback novels, a framed diploma, old packs of gum. But no dictaphones. I repeat the procedure down the road. I'm friendly with the manager of the Alibi Room and he has a garbage bag in the corner of his office filled with lost property. No dice there either. Around the corner, I hit the Little Larder first and, big surprise, I find nothing. It's an upmarket place (lots of lost makeup cases and fancy pens) but it's a dead end. I press on and sort through a plastic bin at the Moray Street Cafe and a cardboard box full of cheap sunglasses and children's toys at the New Farm Deli. Across the river at The Gun Shop, Atomica and a few bars doing a lunch trade, I find piles of library books, busted headphones, socks, video cards, disposable cameras and one hundred black umbrellas.

As the day wears on, I feel as though I'm living in some parallel universe, some other branch of the narrative. Every bit of this crap left behind is a totem of what might have been. Every lone glove, every set of keys, every piece of jewellery, they all represent possibilities foregone. These were choices people made, unwittingly or otherwise. It reminds me of the items discarded by characters in game-books. *Your pack is heavy, you need to dump something. Make the appropriate adjustments to your Equipment List.* These cafe back rooms with their sad little hidey-holes are branches of a story that could have happened, but no one chose them. *If you have the busted headphones, turn to sixty-five.*

Handling this stuff gives me bad ideas. *If Jenny had kept a hold of her fucking dictaphone, would she still be alive today?* I try to stop myself but it's hard not to wonder if there's an alternate timeline out there where something this small saved both of us? It seems insane to marry events like I am but I can't stop. There's always a sequence to things. Connections to be made. Always. That's why I make timelines, because time connects things. Over time, a small thing can lead to a big thing. A small thing can kill you. Given enough time, anything can happen. All sparks become an explosion.

The wrong kiss.

The cell dividing.

One more drink for the road.

Every horrible outcome, all from a seed.

Is the dictaphone Jenny's seed?

Or is it my seed?

Stop.

St—

But I can't stop today.

Did I bully a young woman onto the path that led to her death? I *did*, in some capacity, didn't I? But did I do it in other ways too, ways I'm yet to grasp hold of? Did I unwittingly push the wrong person towards darkness and chaos? Did I invite carnage into my own house? Did I do all this for a dictaphone left on a cafe bench, swept into a back room and dumped in the trash?

What am I really researching here?

The last cafe manager looks at my blank face and says, 'Is it in there?' He checks his watch. We're standing shoulder-to-shoulder in a janitor's closet off an alleyway.

I snap out of my daze.

'No.'

Then I tell him he should throw all this shit in the bin.

★

Jenny's sister, Gloria Wasserman, rents a house on high stilts on Harcourt Street. That's my neighbourhood, it's a half-hour walk from my apartment. Gloria can fill in gaps for me, she may have what I need, but she's not answering the only number I have for her. And no one's answering her door tonight either. The place is closed up tight. I watch from a secluded spot across the street.

A van pulls up.

A woman gets out, straightens a black-and-white tube dress – despite the cold – and starts walking back towards Brunswick Street. I watch her plump arse moving as she walks away. Despite the soaring property prices, the back-streets of New Farm still harbour plenty of street prostitution. It's a messed-up suburb. The million-dollar mansions and sports cars soak up the limelight but in the cracks remain the artists, junkies and hookers of old. It all coexists in some liminal zone between past and present.

My phone vibrates in my pocket.

An unlisted number.

'Hello?'

'Who's this?' A woman's voice.

'Erma Bridges. Who's this?'

'Detective Senior Constable Edwina Packard. I'm returning your call from this morning. Remember me?'

I only have half-formed memories of the police detectives visiting me in the hospital. One of them was an older man, a stockier version of my grandfather in a steel-grey suit. Didn't say much. But the other one was a woman not much older than myself. They were a strange pair. I can vaguely remember the woman turning to the older detective and seeing her ash-blonde hair tucked up in an elaborate bun.

And that's it.

My whole fortnight of bedrest contains about eight hours of crisp memories. I don't know whether it was the shock or the meds but there's not much there. It may well be that I don't want to remember. Tonight, I don't recognise Detective Edwina Packard's face. Only the blonde bun. I'm standing in the interior glare of a Subway restaurant in the bowels of the Myer Centre, looking from customer to customer, when I see the back of her head.

'Detective?'

She glances up, her mouth wrapped around a meatball sub. She coughs, lays the sub down and nods at the empty seat across the table. 'How you doing? You want anything? You can have my cookie.'

'You know, I think I *am* going to get something. Is that weird?'

'What?'

'It just seems . . .'

Edwina reaches into the fob pocket of her pants. 'Here, get me another Diet Coke.'

And so it is that the two of us sit there, eating our sandwiches, talking about the time my research assistant tried to kill me. Edwina launches in with, 'I know it's not what you want to hear but what happened to you is pretty much an open and shut thing. We spoke to everyone. Her parents, her family, her doctors. Your friend was crazy and on drugs. That's the story we heard over and over. That's it, really.' Edwina shrugs. 'People do crazy things when they're high. She was probably trying to rob you. That's all I can say about it.'

'It's not really why I called but . . . I thought she was eccentric. Everyone's a bit that way where I work. I didn't think Jenny was on drugs or manic or anything.'

'She had a history. Maybe she had a good couple of years when you knew her. But let me tell you, the rest of it is pretty messy.'

'Messy how?'

'School complaints, in and out of different places, charges for theft, public nuisance, mostly small stuff, but there's drug convictions and a restraining order in there as well. The family didn't really know how to deal with her. Have you met them?'

'Yeah, some of them. The sister.'

'They've got money, right? They sent her to one shrink after another. In and out of rehab. They did the whole thing that rich people do when their kids screw up. They threw money at the problem.'

'That's really strange,' I say. My parents didn't do that.

Edwina licks one of her fingers. 'How so?'

'Why was she working for me if she had family money?'

'Her parents cut her off. That's what the sister told us. You sure you didn't notice *any* change in Jenny's behaviour towards the end?'

'She was a bit erratic. She wanted money, that's for sure. I guess that adds up. What drug was she on?'

'A lot of different stuff. On the night in question, LSD and ice, mainly. You heard of ice?'

I shake my head.

'It's new. Methamphetamine, like speed. Really really dirty speed. She was messed up. Her blood work . . . She should have been dead. And if you combine that sort of use with a pre-existing mental condition, it's just a matter of time. If it wasn't you, it would have been someone else.'

It was a lot of new information. 'What about the gun? Did you ever work out where that came from?'

'No. That's the real mystery on our end. I'm not really supposed to tell you this but look, it was an older pistol, pre-registration. No one in her family has any history with firearms. No friends or ex-boyfriends. We don't know where it came from. But—' and she leans across the table '—that same gun has killed someone before. Ballistics matched it to a body dumped out in a field in Gatton ten years ago. Someone shot a bikie with it.'

'That's crazy.'

'I know, right. Did Jenny ever mention a bikie gang to you? Banditos? Coffin Cheaters? Doomriders?'

'God, no. Nothing.'

'Good.'

I take a bite of my sandwich.

'Look, don't beat yourself up about it,' says Edwina. 'Some people are lying pieces of shit and they do things that none of us normal people understand. That's what I've learned doing this for a living. What happened to you, it's like getting hit by a bus. You step out, then the wrong person runs you down. That's all it is.'

'I don't know—'

'Nope. You're an academic right? You can't learn anything from this, OK? Just get on with your life. I know it's hard to hear but, honestly, that's the best thing you can do right now. Just try and forget about it. All this bullshit these days, blah, blah, blah *recovery* and blah, blah, blah *closure* and whatever else. It's nonsense. Let me tell you something, *you've* got to forget about this. Just push it down. Keep it out of your mind. If you can do that long enough, it leaves permanently, trust me. All the psycho-babble is just beating around the bush.'

'Sounds like good advice.'

'It is.' Edwina folds her Subway wrapper into a neat rectangle. 'Anything else?'

'Jenny had something of mine. Interview data.'

'Like, numbers or something?'

'Audio files, for my work. I think it's on a dictaphone. Could that be sitting in a box at the station?'

'Maybe. There'll be a package of her stuff somewhere. I'll do you a deal. I'll take a quick look for that dictaphone if you give me your stamps.'

'What stamps?'

'The Subway stamps.'

Two half-inch stamps sit beside a bunched napkin on the table in front of me. I can't even remember taking them from the clerk.

'Deal.'

Detective Edwina leans over and delicately picks up the stamps with a wet fingertip. Close to me now, I can see something behind her ear: a small tattoo, a plain circle of dark ink sitting just beneath the neatly pulled hair.

I open the door to my dark apartment. It's the same as it ever was, except haunted. As I pass my bedroom door there's the voice whispering:

That's where you landed.

That's where she fired the gun.

That's where the blood went.

I ignore it, head straight through to the lounge room and flop down on the couch and stare at the ceiling. I call the cat but the little prick doesn't come. After a time, I see that there's a slight red glow to the room. I scan around. The answering machine blinks.

I push the button.

You have two new messages. The first message, received at three forty-five p.m. Hi, Erma, this is Howard. Someone thought they saw you on campus today. Was that you? If so, and if you're feeling more comfortable about everything, give me a call or drop by the Centre. We'd love to have you back. Just call the office or stop in. Hope you're well.

Click.

Next message, received at seven fifty-eight p.m. —or so I thought. In the beginning, none of us really thought much about

86

the deeper meaning of what we were creating. There was, I guess, a mild sense of the occult floating around. It was the eighties after all, a time of moral panic, the Dungeons & Dragons scare and so on. Anyone who came to gamebooks in that era – came fresh to it, as I did – they had some sense that they were entering a slightly dark place and – oh, sorry – Where was I? Ah, gamebooks, yes, gamebooks; they are, in their own way, a particularly dark place if you really think about it. In role-playing games, the characters pick and choose. They shift the story. They influence things. But in gamebooks, that's locked down. It's control—

Click.

To play the message again, press . . .

I listen again.

I know the voice but I can't accept that I know it. I run to the study and open a video on my computer of Archibald Moder giving an interview on British TV. He's narrow across the shoulders with a neat black beard. An ageing Ben Kingsley. I hit the volume and the room fills with his voice.

Thin, nasally, insistent.

The same voice.

Moder was a psychotherapist before he turned to writing and his interviews are filled with this very precise way of talking to people. He has an unmistakable cadence. A slow deliberate pace that sounds like conversation but is often deeply rhetorical and subjective.

I go back to the machine and play the message five more times.

It's him.

A recording. An answering machine recording of an interview.

I zero in on the message a sixth time, to one particular fragment:

– dark place and – oh, sorry – Where was I?

and – oh, sorry – Where . . .

– oh, sorry –

And there, in that tiny space inside the sentence, I can hear a woman's voice in the background. A gentle laugh as she apologises. I play it again and again and again. Something falls or slips and there she is.

A woman.

A girl.

Jenny.

My legs shake. I reach for the wall and miss.

I crumple up.

SERO

10

You ride the stolen horse for three days across grasslands without end. You follow your map and orient yourself against wells marked with crude windmills. Three days of waist-high pasture brushing against the horse followed by three eerie cloudless nights spent sleeping in the blades. The monotony of it irks you. Even the horse is bothered. The two of you don't speak. You don't reassure the animal. It doesn't seem friendly. Ash grey and angry, is what it is. Tormented. The horse refuses any kind of unnecessary contact and you're both glad for each night's separation.

11

On the fourth day, you ride out of the plains and up into the mountains. A structure appears, stilts and beams protruding up into the sky, a small timber castle built into the mountain wall. Its windows glow.

As you walk the horse into a cobblestone courtyard, two shapes appear, both cloaked in black gowns. Both figures have cherry-red skin. They greet you in a strange tongue.

'I can't understand that.'

'Ah-ha. I told you he was human,' says one of the figures, removing her hood. 'You must have travelled a long way to be this far into Emery.'

'I've come a distance.'

The other one clasps her hands. 'And where are you headed, traveller?'

'A distance yet.'

'Humans are like this,' says the first one. 'They enjoy secrets. I've been told this.'

Her partner nods. 'Do you seek lodgings? Is *that* something you can disclose?'

'What is this place?'

They both smile at that.

'This is Firetop House,' says the shorter one. 'It's whatever you want it to be, if you have gold.'

'I have gold,' you say.

12

One coin buys you everything. You feast on fowl and wine by an open fire. You bathe in hot water, hands reaching in to scrub your skin, working soap through your hair and across your back. As they attend to you, a pale eunuch plays a stringed instrument and it works on you like a potion, closing your eyes for an indeterminate period. Later, you find yourself in a bubbling hot spring with a black sky above. The rain starts to become a sleeting soft ice.

'It's snow,' says your host. 'Have you seen snow before?'

'No. I thought it would be heavier.'

The host waits by the pool until your companions arrive. There are two of them, a man and a woman. As they slip from their gowns the host says something to them in her language and the companions nod in agreement.

The female companion drops into the pool first. She wades across. As she touches you, the softness of her is as startling as the heat from a fire.

The male companion waits on the other side.

He smiles.

The woman kisses your neck, runs a hand across your scalp. The man begins to approach through the water while fingers slip between your legs, and then the man is close and he smells different to the woman, like treated pine. His breath is warm.

His tongue touches your lips.

And you remember something:

Another pool.

Another man.

Another kiss.

The world screams inside your mind for an instant but only until you find yourself engulfed.

ERMA

It's 7.50 a.m. and the Centre for Creative Writing and Cultural Understanding is pretty much as I left it. Kanika is the only person here at this time of day. I knock on the Squadroom glass. She smiles and waves me in. 'The prodigal son returns.'

'We'll see.' The interior of her office is like a flashback. Books in piles. Stacked papers. Wine stains. The wall of shame: the fourteen photographs of missing girls. 'Is this still going?'

'I wrote the book. But it feels weird to take them down, and I've got an ARC grant in for a continuation. I'm working on the examiners' reports at the moment.'

'Sounds good.' I don't know what else to say. I stand there in the doorway trying to think of something.

'Been to your office yet?'

It's the next one over. 'No. I forgot my keys. It's been so long I stopped carrying them.'

'I'll call security. You want a coffee?'

It takes forty minutes for the university security guard to arrive and, when he does, he takes his time testing each master key in the lock, wheezing softly. 'Lot of doors in this place,' he says.

Kanika, who hates these guys with a passion, who wonders out loud what security *actually* do on a university campus with a history of missing women, groans and says, 'This is taking a *long* time, dude.'

The guard stops. 'Hey, I've got these keys and this lock. That's the situation.'

'What if there was a fire?' says Kanika. 'What if something like that happened and we needed to open a door in a hurry?'

'That would be a good day to remember your keys,' says the guard.

Kanika takes out a notebook. 'What's your name?'

'Rob.' He grunts. The lock snaps open. 'There we go.'

I look in. It's all there.

My career on pause.

My old life.

It even smells like it used to.

'Have a good day,' says the guard.

'You too, Rob,' says Kanika, holding up her middle finger as he waddles off.

When I'm alone in my office, in my old office chair, something happens. I shut down. I leave my body. I daydream. I'm not sure where I go. I'm not sure what I'm thinking about but the trance is broken by the phone.

It's Howard's extension.

'You want a coffee?' he says.

★

Howard Chandler might be the only thing that has changed. He's still wearing jeans and trainers to work but his face looks five years older. 'I'm miserable,' he says, more a statement than a complaint. As my eyes adjust to the sunny brightness of his room, I notice his hair is lighter too, greyer. 'Erma, I just can't hack it like I used to.'

'So, things have gotten worse?'

'I've got fucking students, undergrads, using terminology like "job-ready". They talk like the execs these days. Can't tell them apart. I don't know how to feel about it. I never thought that way at uni. Did you?'

'I did a business degree. I think it's obvious I wasn't thinking much of anything when I was in undergrad.'

'How are you, anyway? You coming back?'

'I guess.'

'You need anything? You might have to pick up some teaching next semester, just till we get things squared away.'

'That's fine. Do I still have to do something about those complaints?'

'It's still ongoing, I'm afraid. I can't say I'm surprised. We didn't dodge that bullet while you were away, not entirely . . . Sorry.'

'It's OK.'

'You sure?'

'What are you asking me?'

Howard rubs at his right eye with his palm. 'Are you OK, Erma? It's fucked up. It's really fucked up what happened to you.'

'I'm fine, Howard.'

He nods but I can tell he doesn't believe me.

I spend the day deleting emails. I hit the campus gym. I work on my cross. It's getting better. The dint where my fist piles into the bag is much narrower and deeper now. I still look the same. There's still a softness to my face, to my eyes especially. I don't look like an imposing person. Never have. But when I track back across to this black punching bag, I know that it's absolutely gotten to the point where I wouldn't want to be hit by me.

I head home but end up back on Harcourt Street. I find a parking spot near Jenny's sister's place, then grab a noodle box and bring it back to the car, back to the half-arsed stakeout I've promised myself is actually about rebooting my career and not about Jenny.

I eat and watch Gloria's empty house. She's still refusing to return my calls. As the evening darkens, a harsh wind roars around me, rocking the car. Nothing else happens. After three hours, I start the car and pull into Gloria's driveway to make a U-turn, my headlights pushing through the timber latticework at the bottom of the house. The wind is violently lifting and dropping something inside. I roll down the window and listen. A tarpaulin. A sustained blast has the thing flapping and bellying so high it raps the undercarriage of the house.

I check the rear-view. Everyone's indoors. The street is dead.

I get out.

The front door to Gloria's garage is locked with a chain but I circle round the house and find a laundry with an earth floor. The laundry leads through to the garage from behind. As I step in, the tarp roars up and there in the fractured beams of my headlights is Jenny's car, caked in dust.

This feels wrong.

Just push it down.

I try the driver's side door: locked.

The wind blasts again.

A rope is attached to a free corner of the tarp. It whips past my face and I blink. *Shit.* Almost had my eye. The air sucks back in and the car is covered over again. Spooked, I back out.

I try to sleep but can't go deep enough to dream.

3.03 a.m.

I get out of bed without really deciding to.

Boil the jug.

Pace the carpet in the hallway, waiting.

My laptop is open on the coffee table, already on. I kid myself that I'm starting the day early and check my email. I have eighty-five new emails since I left the office last night. The first is a call-for-papers for a popular culture conference on Britney Spears and Paris Hilton. *Papers that touch on the Britney/Paris continuum as collective desire, objects of fandom, an embodiment of—*

Delete.

Second message:

Dora Bridges has published a new blog post on Myspace. Click the link below to read the post . . .

My sister.

I hit the URL and a blue box of text appears on the screen. Dora has a few Myspace profiles, each different in terms of style or theme or whatever. On this one, she writes in block capitals. I don't know why my sister does this stuff. No one does. Her life is always half fantasy. On this account, she posts the same type of missive each time: short, vague debriefs that look like poems.

> *SINCE HE LEFT I CAN BREATHE AGAIN.*
> *3 MONTHS NOW. CAN'T BELIEVE IT.*
> *PHILIPPA STILL CALLS OUT FOR HIM IN*
> *THE NIGHT AND IT BREAKS MY HEART.*
> *A COLD WINTER BUT GETTING BETTER.*
> *HOPE YR WELL.*
> *XOX*
> *D*

The details of this race through my blood like a drug. *He left?* HE is her husband, Euan. *Her ex-husband now?* No way of knowing. My family is a mess. Dad calls me three times a year. Mum calls when she wants something. And I haven't spoken to Dora this century. We can't be together. Don't belong together. We aren't really sisters.

I get so wound up by Dora's message that exercise is the only option. I take to the streets. I run. I have to. The fact that I'm running back towards Gloria's house – to Jenny's car under Gloria's house – with a backpack containing a crowbar wrapped in a bath towel, it's almost a side note.

Just push it down.

Just push . . .

I hear Detective Edwina on loop with:

– dark place and – oh, sorry – Where was I?
and – oh, sorry – Where . . .
– oh, sorry –

'Stop,' I whisper between breaths, but things are at a point where I'm not entirely sure who I'm talking to.

A police car glides past as I come into the long crescent of Moray Street. *It's fine. It's just a crowbar, wrapped in a bath towel.* The headlight passes over me and the street returns to pre-dawn near-dark.

Growing up, we had a swimming pool in the serviced lawn behind our house. My parents heated it during the winter. We were that sort of family. Lived in a six-bedroom manse behind green hedges. A circular drive, marble floors, the whole bit. You're not supposed to come from this sort of money in my profession. Cultural studies is academia for the working class. And yet I'm none of these things, not in my bones.

At least my parents didn't inherit their wealth. Dad was a second-generation Brit and his family washed up in Melbourne with next to nothing. He put himself through business school and started his first management gig at twenty-three after a stint clerking somewhere. That first job was where he met my mother. Mum started out as a receptionist but retrained in accounting as soon as Dad got rolling. She owns a franchise of gift shops now.

I was born when my mother was twenty-seven. My sister is eleven months younger. Irish twins, as they say.

Growing up it was clear to Dora and I that our parents made their money the hard way, that making it took time, and that this was how it was done. They would come and go from the house at all hours – Dad away for weeks at a time. What I now view as a type of neglect was just the 'cost of doing business'. That's ultimately what our family was. 'We have to work together,' my mother would say.

She doesn't say it anymore.

I kind of blew that up.

The ground drops away on Annie Street and I go with it, running faster, leaning in. I cut across Clay and take Heal down to James Street, passing the last gasp of suburbia (the school, the butcher) and turning into the bottom of Harcourt. There's a prostitute standing on the sidewalk and we nod at each other as I pass.

My sister had a car accident in August of '99. She was driving someone across town in her cream BMW sedan, a birthday present from my dad. It was a bright day. Eleven o'clock. An old man with the sun in his eyes rammed into her driver's side, pushing her car across an intersection and into a light pole.

Dora was pretty banged up. Broken arms and leg, whip-lash, bedridden for weeks. I had to look after her. Dad was away. Mum was opening a new store. For weeks I did everything for Dora. I cleaned her, fed her, kept her company. Dora's boyfriend Euan was around but he was hopeless. He spent his days 'helping out' as if on vacation. He lounged around the house watching TV, practising his golf swing (he played twice a week already, at twenty-five) and broke that up with beer and long swims in the family pool. He was *supposed* to be attending to the yard as well as Dora. That's what my mother paid him for. He was the fucking gardening guy, originally. But he evolved into something else once he started dating my sister.

After three weeks with a bedridden Dora, I started to hate everyone. I had my own problems. I was already well and truly depressed when my sister had her accident. The shock of almost losing her piled on top of the toxic experience of having her around all the time, at her worst – it crushed me. She was horrible to everyone: a demanding, angry victim. It was the worst couple of months of my life.

One night, Dora's sobbing echoed through the house and I officially gave up. She'd had some sort of fight with Euan – she was even more mean to him than me, I should add – and instead of going in to clean up the plate of half-finished food she'd hurled across the room, I tiptoed down to the kitchen and made my way to the pool. Under the lukewarm water, I let the real black tar feelings run their course. And then someone else slipped into the water.

I take a breather under a Frangipani tree across the street from Gloria's house. The place is still closed up like before. I put my gloves on. They're the only ones I have: two yellow and green dishwashing gloves.

I creep across the bitumen.

Around the house.

Through the rear laundry.

Into the garage.

Jenny's car sits there under the tarpaulin. No headlights or wind now. I unwrap the crowbar and slide it into the seam of the driver's side door. The first moment of metal touching metal squeaks loud. The neighbours can hear it, if they're up. I figure my best bet is to go fast. I yank on the crowbar and the door pops.

You have two minutes.

The passenger seat is covered in clothes and plastic shopping bags filled with coffee cups and food wrappers. My hands dart across all of it, squeezing items, groping for the cold hard plastic of a dictaphone. I don't find it. I scramble over into the back and pull down the bench seats and crawl halfway into the boot. It smells like mildew and sweat and I can't see a thing but I claw at books, shoes, a rubber raincoat. From there, I check under all the seats and, with my eyes properly adjusted to the interior, I scan the centre console and dash. Nothing. I open the glovebox and pray for a miracle. In return, I get something so puzzling I almost yelp in fright as I draw it out.

A leather gun holster.

Inside the holster, a greasy dildo wrapped in a freezer bag.

What the hell?

I shove both in my pack and pad around in the glovebox,

dragging out a tattered street directory. That goes in my pack as well. And then I'm out on James Street, jogging faster than I'd like. It's two full blocks later before I remember the gloves. I'm still wearing them.

When I was ten, my mother developed a strange hobby: holding her breath underwater. It started with a documentary on Filipino free divers – she was importing something from the Philippines for the shop – and soon holding her breath became something she experimented with in the en suite bath, then the family pool. Everyone told her to stop doing it. But my mother never listens. I suppose we're both a bit like that.

One day, Dad sends me downstairs to fetch Mum for dinner and there she is at the bottom of the pool, floating gently. As soon as I saw her, I knew she was in danger. Felt it. I lunged in and dragged her out. I pushed my breath into her lungs and screamed for help, pumped her chest. I was working on her with such determination that the ambulance officers had to prise me off her.

I wouldn't let go.

I had to save her.

I *did* save her.

And the fortnight that followed was one of the brightest of my life. The rewards I received for saving my mother's life – attention from my father, a write-up in the local paper, a little award from the Victorian Ambulance Service – and the pride I felt, it was so good and pure.

I was a hero.

I'm ashamed to admit how little of my adult life has married up to that moment. Years later, I wonder if that heroic impulse truly resides within me – deep, deep down – or if I was just a dumb kid who did what any other dumb kid would have done in that situation? It was my mother. Dying. That's biology, right?

Jenny's stuff bounces around in my pack as I run the path along the Brisbane River to Moray Street. I don't know why I'm here, searching for breath with this fucked-up inventory:

Crowbar.

Bath towel.

Street directory.

Dildo.

Gun holster.

But it reminds me of that thing with my mum and the house and my sister. I'm stretched. I'm acting like that again. Angry. Impulsive. Diving in.

By morning, my kitchen timeline of Jenny's last days has new notches on it. The weirder items I stole from her car don't tell me a lot. The dildo is iridescent purple and bigger than anything I'd ever want inside me but nothing else about it is remarkable. There's no clue in it. The leather gun holster isn't much better. It tells me two things: one, the gun may have belonged to someone called Simon because that name is written in marker on the side of the thing, and two, the police haven't searched Jenny's car. I figure they'd be interested in the holster.

What *is* useful is Jenny's street directory. It's marked up with all sorts of annotations, most of them matching up to dates and meetings on my timeline. Yet there's one page and one address that doesn't appear anywhere else. It's a page showing the backstreets of Kelvin Grove. The directory falls open to it, like Jenny used the page all the time, and there's a Post-it note affixed:

CRAIG
10 Woolcock Street

I don't know a Craig.

There's no Craig on the timeline.

I put in an early-morning appearance at the Centre because I want to feel like a person who goes to work every day. I sit in my office. Drink coffee. Delete emails. I call the other missing interview respondents Jenny lost to the void. They all tell a similar story: *she was nice, she asked me questions about my collection of gamebooks, she stopped by and talked about my writing.* No one remembers anything except for how she looked and roughly when she arrived. It's a relief in a way. No one spotted a drug addict or a crazy person. I wasn't a complete fool, it seems. When I'm done, I follow up with Archibald Moder. No one picks up, but when his answering machine clicks in, I repeat my story: *the girl who interviewed you last winter passed away violently and I'd like to speak with you regarding this matter.* Another lie. I don't want to talk to anyone about Jenny. But sometimes a lie is the thing one needs most.

Craig's house is an old timber place built into the slope of Woolcock Street. There's a garage below street level and I can hear music reverberating out. I follow the sound. It's something with guitars. Can't place it. As I move under the house, I see that the garage is empty bar for a lawnmower, an old couch and some packing boxes, but out back there's a fire in a shallow pit and a man

106

sitting beside the fire. He has a stereo propped up on an old chair.

'Hello?'

He doesn't hear me.

I move about halfway along the house. 'Hello?'

'Out here.'

'Craig?' I say, stepping into the yard. There's no garden. Just a Hills Hoist and a path and a line of sad, struggling trees right up the far end. Other than that, there's dying grass and this fire pit.

Craig – I think it's him – nods, a joint smouldering in his hand. He's about my age, a bit older maybe, and not presentable at all. He's wearing a faded collared shirt barely containing a round beer gut, and this over dirty black denim cut-offs and filthy uncovered feet. He looks like a business student gone to seed.

'Who are you?' he says.

'I'm a friend of Jenny's.'

'Oh, right.' He takes a toke.

'Are you allowed to have a fire out in the open?'

'Yeah, I think so.'

'What *is* this?' I nod in the direction of the music.

'The Veronicas.'

'Christ. Can I turn it down?'

He shrugs. 'Hey, can I ask you something?'

I sit on a spare chair beside him. 'Shoot.'

'Where is Jenny? Haven't see her in ages. Have you seen her?'

'Not in a while.'

'So, why are you, you know, here? Does she need something? I just . . . you know.'

'What?'

'She can't send people here for shit if she's buying her regular stuff somewhere else. That's not how it works.'

'She told me you were her boyfriend.' I'm proud of this improvisation, even as I say it. This is exactly the sort of lie Jenny would tell people and it works on Craig. He coughs out a lungful of smoke and flicks the roach into the fire.

'What!'

The cough turns into a fit of barking and spitting. As he calms down, I hear a window slide open behind us. A woman hangs her head out and says, 'Babe, you gotta get that looked at.'

'Yeah, OK. *OK.*'

'Who's this?' says the woman.

'I'm a friend of Jenny's.'

'Doesn't that cunt owe you money, babe?'

Craig says, 'Carrie, go back inside, all right?'

'Why?'

'Just fuckin' like, go back in. I gotta—'

The window slams shut.

'*That's* my girlfriend,' he says.

'So, Jenny was lying?'

'Kinda. What do you . . . what do you want?'

'Did Jenny leave anything here? I'm looking for a dictaphone.'

'A dick phone? What's that?'

'It's . . . She never stayed here, right?'

Craig actually moves for the first time. He comes closer, stands over me. 'What's she been saying, like, exactly?'

I ignore it. 'Can you sort me out with something?'

He grabs my arm and yanks me. 'Where is she?'

'Let me go.'

Craig twists my arm. I struggle, pull away from him, but only to open him up. While he's distracted, I come over with the other hand, my right fist whipping down into the side of his head. Craig recoils like he's been stung by a wasp. He lets go but tries to straighten up too quickly. As he's staggering sideways, I jab him again, in his side. In a split second he's on the ground and I'm on top of him, my hand threaded with a fistful of his hair. I don't know what I'm doing. We don't grapple in Muay Thai. We don't get on the ground like this.

This is all me.

'How do you know Jenny? Tell me or I'll hit you again.' I pump my fist tight and feel his scalp flex a little.

'Fuck, fuck. I just sold gear to her, OK? Let me go.'

'What sort of gear?'

'Ice. Speed. Whatever I could . . . agh . . . get my hands on. Fuck.'

'Who hooked you two up?' I hit him again, just to get it over with. 'Tell me.'

'No one.'

'Craig!'

'No one. She just rocked up here one night like you.'

'You know she nearly killed someone on that stuff you gave her?'

'What?' He starts coughing and sucking in fast asthmatic breaths. I let him up and he scrambles back a few feet.

'Tell me everything you remember about her.'

'Nah, I don't remember nothing.'

'Come on, Craig,' I say, following him. We both hear someone running through the house behind us. I catch his eye and say, 'I'll hurt her too.'

'Look, look, she was a stripper and shit, right? That's it. Jenny came to me for stuff to keep her up at night. Said she had to work all the time. That's all. Fuck. That's it!'

'Where'd she work?'

'Sam Hell.'

I know it. A notorious Valley haunt. *New information.* A door slams behind me. I look over my shoulder and this Carrie woman is running across the yard towards me, holding a kitchen knife.

I point at her and shout, 'Stop. *Stop.* Think about it.'

Carrie stops running. She looks at Craig snivelling on the ground. She looks at me.

'You stay there, he's stays there, I walk away, OK?'

Carrie nods.

As I pass her I tell her. 'You're too smart for this guy.'

In the car, a block from Craig's house, my arms start to shake so bad I have to pull over. My right hand is swelling up. I unbuckle the seat belt. Tree branches overhead, flickering afternoon light. The walls of the car contract around me.

I close my eyes.

Rapid-fire memories.

Flash.

Flash.

Flash.

I start crying. Huffing breaths in and out like Craig. I dive into the back seat. I scream into the seams.

SERO

13

A path stretches along the mountain range, across snow-covered ledges and down tunnels dug into the rock. The descent takes you deep inside a canyon, a day's ride from the mountain summit to the canyon floor. At the end of the gorge, you find the entrance to a gated city. On your map, this is a place called Ulteron.

From the outside, Ulteron is a cluttered mass of rooftops and spires set behind a siege wall that spans the full width of the canyon. There is a large iron gate. You line up behind a motley collection of soldiers – all of them drunk and covered in melted snow.

When it's your turn, the clerk grunts out a greeting.

'Purpose?' he says.

'I've come about a priest. I'm without memory.'

'We've all sorts of priests in here.'

You turn your map over. Sister Rhys has written the word there.

'Rohank.'

'Hold on.' The clerk steps back from his window. A

minute later, he reappears. 'How much gold do you have?'

They take a deposit, something to be forfeited should you cause harm, or find it, in the city. When it's done, you stand with the soldiers and wait for the gate to rise. As it inches up, one of the men winks at you.

14

At least as far as you remember, Ulteron is like no place you've set foot before. All nature and wildness are removed from view. Within the walls, it is like one giant building cut from stone and concrete. A bustling maze. Very narrow and flat. The horse isn't fond of it. It's the first thing you agree on.

Hungry, you seek out an inn and find one with a stable. For a small coin, you buy ale and lodging. The innkeeper's wife shows you to your room. As she turns down the bed, you tell her you're looking for the priest called Rohank.

She shakes her head. 'He's not one to fuss with.'

'Can you direct me?'

'Saint Rohank lives above the rest of us, dear. He's not a poor man. You'd have to ask the local mob for an invitation. There's a church down the street.'

You look out the window. A group of boys travel the street lighting lanterns. No sign of a church.

'It's down some,' the innkeeper's wife adds. 'You know,

113

they say Rohank can see into a person's heart. It's a terrible business. I wouldn't go within a hundred paces of him.'

After she leaves, you tend to your belongings:

The sword.

The stolen clothes.

The charcoal map.

The yellow vial.

After a time, you grow weary of the room and decide to try the church despite the hour.

15

The church at the end of the road is one of the few buildings in the city that sits apart from the others. Stationed in a cobblestone courtyard, the little brick building has an eerie presence. Nothing decorative about it. If not for the doors and signage, one could mistake it for a shed or furnace. The inside is more ornate. Gilded walls, velvet drapes. Dozens of glowing candles. Rows of timber pews polished to the point of reflection. And yet, the ominous feel of the exterior remains. This is not a good place.

At the front of the room, an old man waits by an elaborate black booth. As you walk down the centre aisle, he disappears behind a curtain on the side of the booth and a low murmur floats out. A minute later, the old man reappears, bows to the altar and shuffles past.

'Yes?' says a voice. It comes from the booth.

'Who goes there?'

The curtain parts and a weathered Elven face peers out. An old nun. She wears a black garment around her head, obscuring her hair and ears. 'Speak, tell me.'

'I come searching for the one they call Rohank.'

'And what do you want with him?'

'I need magic performed.'

'That's not our way. Come closer.' The nun's sharp black eyes scan the length of you as you near. 'Rohank won't see you in this state. Step inside here. I'll hear your confession, then we can talk more about my brother and his treatments.'

'What is this confession you speak of?'

'Confess to the gods all ye who carry a burden,' she says, and, reading your face, she adds, 'You tell me all the bad things you've done.'

'In return for what?'

'Purity. A blessing.'

'Does it work?'

'Of course it works. This is what we do all day. Now, come in here.'

The nun closes the curtain to her side of the chamber. You reluctantly cram yourself into the small compartment adjoining it. As your eyes adjust to the darkness, you spot the nun's silhouette in the small grilled portal. She incants something in an ancient language, something almost completely alien to you, but you pick up the odd word. *Acknowledge. Conceal. Prosper.* In the plain language she says, 'Speak now of your transgressions.'

'I woke in a cave. I have no memory from a time before that.'

'Yes, yes, but have you broken the directives of the gods?'

'I do not know these rules.'

'Have you killed?'

'Yes. Many. Both orc and man.'

'Did you steal that which belongs to others?'

'Can you steal from the dead?'

'You can.'

'Then yes, I've stolen gold, equipment and livestock.'

'Have you lain with one outside of marriage?'

'I have.'

'Does any of this weigh on your mind?'

'No.'

'No? Not at all?'

'I've overworked my horse. It's a beast of a thing, but it deserves better. I feel bad about the horse.'

'Did you beat it with fist or branch?'

'No.'

'Did you lay with it?'

'What?'

'Did you lay with your horse.'

'I did not. It's not a well-tempered animal.'

'Good. Do you acknowledge the gods?'

You remember something. It comes fast. A flickering memory.

Muscles strained.

Humid air.

A roar of eternal damnation.

I of unlord, I of—

'What is it?' says the nun.

'Might I be without the gods?'

The nun clears her throat. 'That is a very dark question. Answer me this and think very carefully before answering.' She clears her throat. When she speaks again, her voice sounds different, sinister, almost ghoulish. 'Who hunts in the dead of night?'

You answer without thought. 'A woman.' The nun's voice is like a trance or potion working through you.

'Who swallows the tide when no tide comes?' says the nun.

'She does.'

What is this? The booth tightens. Your nails dig into your palms.

'Who binds the names to the nameless one?'

'The woman. The woman does,' you hear yourself say.

'Do you seek her out?'

'I must. I'm here.'

'You can rest now.'

You escape the booth. 'What is this witchcraft?' you scream. 'Who is this *woman* you force me to speak of?'

'Be calm,' says the nun. Her natural voice has

returned. She steps out of the booth, gathering her robes around her legs. She is short, even for an elf, her head barely reaches the height of your waist. 'Come. I'll take you to Rohank. He's been waiting for one such as you.' She takes one more look at you. 'Yes,' she says. 'Yes, yes.'

ERMA

After what happened with Craig, I try to keep things steady. I go to work. I go home. I go to the gym. For four days, it's all a straight line, a clear vector. Back to my to-do lists and calendars. And for four days – days that feel like weeks – there are no interruptions. No one hits up my answering machine with creepy messages. No one mentions my year away or the *incident*. By Day Four, the hand I busted on Craig works again and there's no word from him. *He probably doesn't even remember what hit him.* That's what I tell myself.

But then I slip.

An afternoon meeting with David Brier gets to me. He's on the final draft of his thesis. He seems to have thrived without my supervision. It irks me. After I give him my notes, he rolls a cigarette in my office and says, 'Fancy a beer?' We start at the UQ staff bar. The second glass goes straight to my head and I blow off training for the night. David mentions a show upstairs at the Shamrock Hotel and after pizza we take the bus in to the Valley together. It's after we get off the bus, as I draw money from an ATM, that he notices my bandaged hand.

'How'd you do that?'

I'm tipsy so I tell him the truth. 'I had to hit a guy.'

'What? Why?'

'Just had to.'

'You mean, a guy attacked you? Were you walking alone?'

'Doesn't matter. And I never walk alone.' I hold up my fists. 'I've got these.'

David screws up his face.

I shadow-box him like a drunk girl, showing no form at all. I guess I'm flirting. 'Even the devil is the lord of the flies,' I tell him.

David likes that and everything is going fine until he stops walking and says, 'Remember when you asked me about Jenny? This is the spot where we got into that shouting match. This is the spot right here.'

'What are you talking about?' I say, slapping his arm.

We're outside the Fortitude Valley train station. An encampment of junkies and crazies line the pavement, hitting up the suburban drunks as they stagger out into the cold.

David doesn't seem to notice the rabble. 'Last year, when you were looking for Jenny, you asked me about the last time I saw her. It was right here.'

I can feel the facade slipping.

Just push it . . .

'Let's keep going.'

David doesn't hear me. 'I was standing here where I am now, finishing a smoke. Jenny was right over there, out on

120

that footpath where those girls are now. Right here is the last time I saw her. She was screaming, "Fuck you man, fuck! You!" It was like months had been erased or something because she was screaming about you as well. Isn't that strange? It's crazy strange. I thought her and I were over our weirdness by then, but obviously not. That was, like, eighteen months ago now. It feels like, damn, it feels raw now, know what I mean?'

Feels raw? For you?

I look across the street. Two skinny girls in black tube dresses stand outside a grimy club entrance. The glowing sign above them reads Sam Hell. A strip club. It's the name I beat out of Craig.

I say to David, 'I've got to go.'

I act as if I'm heading home but really I circle around for a cheap takeaway coffee (to sober me up) then back through the Chinatown Mall and along Wickham Street to Sam Hell. The same two skinny girls are still outside. There's a 'Dancers Wanted' sign in the window. I walk up to the man on the door and say, 'I want to talk to the boss.'

The truth about Fortitude Valley is that it's worse in the mornings. Friday and Saturday nights are full of routine street violence – men beating up men in cab lines and dark corners – but the weeknights are fairly calm. You could go down there at nine o'clock on a Tuesday night and leave with the impression that the Valley isn't much more than a dirtier iteration of Brisbane's retail district. No, the real collision happens in the mornings, between five and nine. That's when the dark parts of the Valley reappear – the deranged and the random – and those elements slam straight into the early morning commuters and New Farm joggers. Five to nine are the witching hours. It's a bad sign that the owner of Sam Hell wants to meet me at 8.45 a.m.

The door to Sam Hell opens. A woman pops her head out. 'Erma?'

I gave them my real name. I don't know why.

The woman leads me down to the club floor. The house lights are on and in the bright fluorescence the place has the ambience of an Elizabethan-themed porn film. Burgundy carpets, mist rising up from a recent steam clean.

Gold-rimmed mirrors. The timber and brass furniture that might pass for refined in the dark is sad and chipped.

'Over here,' says the woman. She takes me across the dance floor to a set of long deep booths. In one of the booths, a man – mid-fifties, receding grey hair, red polo shirt – eats McDonald's from a paper bag. Across from him is a girl with the body and face of a fifteen-year-old. In the next booth along, there are three big men, all in black shirts, just sitting there.

'Morning,' says the man in the polo shirt. 'I'm Roberto and this is Kylie. That's right, isn't it, love?'

'Carla,' says the girl. Her eyes are pinned. Up close, she's older than she looks but not by much. Late teens, at a stretch.

'Right, right. Carla and Erma. I like it. So, have you two worked in clubs before?'

Carla nods. 'I do Thursdays at Bad Girls.'

'OK, sure.' He turns to me. 'Don't take this personally, love, but you don't look like much of a dancer. You done this before? Stand up again and let me have a look at you.'

'I'm not here for a job.'

'No?'

'I spoke to someone last night. I had some questions about—'

'No questions,' says Roberto. 'What the fuck is this?'

'All I want is,' and I unfold my picture of Jenny. It's been in my hand the whole time. 'This girl. I'm looking for this girl.'

The room goes quiet. The men in the next booth are listening now. Roberto leans over and snatches the photo from my hand. Stares at it. 'Yes?' he says.

'She has something of mine.'

He looks at me. No answer.

'She's called Jenny. Worked here about eighteen months ago. Do you have a lost property bin or something like that?'

While Roberto continues to stare at the photo, one of the other men steps out. He puts himself off to my side, slightly behind me. I turn and we lock eyes for a moment. I recognise the look.

Roberto breathes out. 'We don't do—'

'I'm just looking for a dictaphone,' I say, panicking. 'That's all. That's it.'

'The fuck,' screams Roberto and the photograph hits me first, followed by a hail of litter from his McDonald's breakfast. 'The fuck! Don't interrupt!'

Carla squeaks. Hot tea leaches into my shirt. Then there's a knife. Roberto has a blade in his hand, catching the light. Hands drag me out of the booth.

'You ever come down here again, I'll open you up,' shouts Roberto, waving the blade around.

I struggle with the hands.

A quieter voice says, 'Stop moving goddamnit,' and by some miracle I stop before I'm punched.

'Get her the fuck out of here!'

Then we're all moving – across the dance floor, past the

bar, up the stairs – moving until my head and shoulders slam into a wall and the wall hinges open. There's daylight behind it. The ground rises up and rough jagged concrete rips my palms as I roll across the pavement. The doors to Sam Hell slam shut behind me.

I can't breathe.

Can't focus.

There's a woman in a business suit standing three metres from me, waiting for a bus, a cigarette hanging from her mouth. 'Fuck,' I snarl through my teeth. '*Fuck.*' The woman averts her eyes.

After Sam Hell, I'm angry. *Throwing* me out of there, onto my fucked-up hand – it doesn't put me off.

Quite the opposite.

It gets my back up and if anything, it makes the whole thing real. Whatever the hell Jenny got into at the club, it feels like a part of the violence she visited on me. A piece of the overall picture. It's the only thing that feels remotely close to what happened between us. The transition Jenny made, that *could* have happened in Sam Hell. In my mind, there's an overlapping vibe. There's an explanation lurking. And it fits my kitchen wall timeline as well. It puts a place to a very specific period, that serves a very specific end. Because there's another thing about the Valley worth mentioning: it's still part-owned by the Queensland mafia, the Agrioli family. When I look up the club, I find very little at first. But when I search for

125

the owner 'Roberto' and add 'Agrioli' I get hits. I get his photo.

The *Courier Mail* tells me Roberto Agrioli did a four-year stretch in Boggo Road Gaol (receiving stolen goods) and came out September 1984. Then there are mentions of him during the Fitzgerald Inquiry. During the dark eighties, he manages the Summer Nights brothel up on McLachlan Street with his brother Joe, a real big shot in the family. Roberto escaped Fitzgerald by the skin of his teeth but went back to the clink anyhow in 1992. Extortion and minor drug possession.

Back out in 2000.

Still out in 2004.

And around Jenny.

'That's about it,' I say to myself. This is the sort of guy who could get her a gun or have one lying around. This all makes sense for the first time. I call Detective Edwina and leave a message.

Days pass. I train. I show my face at the office. I follow up calls and emails. I dodge David Brier. I delete an email from the UQ Conduct Committee, subject line: 'Outstanding Disciplinary Action #2584'. I wait for a call back from the police or from Archibald Moder or his people. With no fresh leads on my Dictaphone, I sit tight and the idleness makes things worse.

Just push it down . . .

— dark place and — oh, sorry — Where was I?

'I'll hurt her too.'

It all circles around like a roulette ball ready to drop into my memories of that night with Jenny:

Why did she fucking do it?

Why did she try to kill me?

Why did she kill herself?

You don't die for me.

And I sense something worse deep down. Some larger truth in the muck. I pace my apartment, awake all day and night, unable to fight back the anxiety, the motion blur, the seasickness. I am a barbarian wandering a foreign land like the one in my dreams. Sero. I keep coming back to that vision of the ocean creature, the giant squid from Thailand. The sickly white eyes in its face. The brown-green tentacles and the tightness of them wrapping around my arms, pulling me in. It feels as real as concrete.

One night, as I'm staring at the timeline on my kitchen wall, I realise I can't remember how long I've been standing there. Minutes? Hours? I'm snapped out of the daze by a new connection, a thought so jarring I actually look around for an intruder or the cat.

Where am I on this timeline?

I imagine the line retreating back past July 2004. I see glowing markers going way back, off the wall into the air. I can sense chaos back there. My own internal chaos mixed in with Jenny's recent trouble, bringing us together, fated. Because we all have parts of ourselves that we don't want to deal with. We all have things we did or failed to do. We all have the stories we choose to tell ourselves in order to live. Our mistakes are always born of these lies. Did my own delusions have a hand in bringing Jenny to my door? Should my faults be on this timeline too? Is there some unconscious lockbox inside myself that explains what happened? Or am I blaming the victim?

My hand aches.

My head hurts, eyes burning.

Sleep deprived.

I look up to the ceiling and imagine the squid sitting

above me, like a decorative ornament on an antique map, overseeing all this.

Its tentacles slide down the wall.

Christ.

I think I'm losing my fucking mind.

SERO

16

The nun shuffles along quickly. She weaves through the city, tut-tutting at your clumsiness as she ducks under carriageways and slips through narrow cobblestone corridors. 'Come on.'

'Where are we going?'

She points to the skyline above.

'Is Rohank in the sky?'

The nun stops. She takes a small pouch from the folds of her robes and fusses with it. She licks her hand, then carefully takes your hand and places a speck of something on the palm. 'Take this. It'll keep you awake. And it'll help with the dark.'

The crystal material is without taste but the poison surges through your arms and legs almost immediately. The night sharpens.

'It's good stuff, isn't it?' says the nun. 'You'll see it all with a clear heart now.'

You look back up into the sky and see a dark brick tower looming over the city.

Crystal magic.

The devil's work.

'How long to reach it?'

'An hour or so. You want another piece of medicine?'

You take it.

17

The nun says, 'Careful now. The path is slight here.' You travel along together, your feet on slimy cobblestones and wet dirt. The nun follows a wall around a large circular pool and into a pitch-black stone corridor. The darkness takes on a slight ochre hue. You can see in it, like a cat.

The nun guides you up a staircase, through a series of hallways. She is still moving quickly, taking almost no note of her surroundings. She knows this passage well. Eventually, you come to a strange timber antechamber lit by torchlight. There is an iron gate set in the wall. The nun goes to the gate and yells something unintelligible into the void beyond.

A fat bearded elf appears on the other side. He nods.

'Calm now,' says the nun.

The whole antechamber shakes.

'What horror is—'

'Calm,' snaps the nun.

The floor emits a loud grinding din and the entire room begins to rise. This is surely the drug because a floating room such as this cannot exist in the human world.

'This will take time,' says the nun.

She carefully sits in her robes. She closes her eyes.

The fear and the drug keep you alert. What could be minutes pass like hours until the room slows and the ceiling comes to rest against a hard surface.

The nun opens her eyes. She points to the iron gate. 'You go through there alone. May the afterworld remain vacant of you.'

'Is it safe?'

'Do you seek safety?' She pushes you. 'Go, now. And, in future, try not to be a blight on the world.'

You draw your sword and step through the gate into a red hallway. The hallway opens out onto a space vast enough to occupy the entire circumference of the tower. There are no torches or candles. Only the drug allows you to see. In the centre of the room, there is a bed and a chair – a bulky piece of furniture, slightly raised, a throne – and on the throne, in the darkness, sits a figure.

'Rohank?'

The figure raises a hand. 'It is I.' His voice is like the vile croak of a toad. 'Who are you?'

'I'm without name.'

'Ahhhh. Come closer then.'

The details of Rohank come into focus as you approach. He is completely naked. A two-score man with a pale short beard and the arms and torso of a soldier. His eyes shine like jewels. Two horrible pink sparks.

'Of the spiral,' he says. 'Interesting. Strange to see one such as yourself this deep into Emery.'

'The spiral?'

'The tattoo on the other side of you. Do not play with me, barbarian. Do you remember receiving these markings?'

'No. That's why I'm here. I've been told you can help restore memories.'

'Have you now? I can't mend you. Only the spiral mends your sort. But I guess I can help. You must need it if you've come all this way to see me. I take it the sister tested you.'

'She asked her questions.'

Rohank lowers his head. 'And you answered?'

'Yes.'

'That's a lie.'

You can't argue it. 'Something answered with my voice.'

'OK, then,' he says.

Without warning, a disturbing sensation wraps itself around your body like a gust of hot wind. The room tightens. To your horror, you watch as an orb of light emerges from Rohank's chest, morphing, stretching out, becoming a pulsing beam. Raw terror blasts through your veins but your body is paralysed as the beam wraps itself around you.

You rise into the air.

This is surely the end of this life.

Driven and burning.

To rise beyond . . .

What is this?

Rohank speaks with demonic clarity, the sound like a spear through your eye, *Thee of suicide, thee of unlord, open thyself to me. I can see you, inside you, staring through.*

'What is this terror I seek?' you say but you are not in control.

The room begins to strobe.

Light sparks.

Red.

White.

Red.

White.

Re—

Total darkness.

Fading glare.

Heat.

Sand.

Wind.

Flying over a desert now, past the walled city into the night and down into dark blood-red sand and through it to passages of coded language and numerology and through further to the arteries of some subterranean world and then, into a lake of cold dark water.

Black water.

Endlessness.

Rohank screams into your mind:

Go under.

Dora. Dora. Dora.

This is your heart, barbarian! Inherit your life!

Dora. Dora. Dora.

Your truth, your memories, your history, your life, it is not of this world and this is the portal.

GO UNDER!

GO TO DORA!

Rohank laughs, clearly insane. His voice echoes around the room.

Speak clearly to Dora, barbarian. Speak clear—

'The . . .'

What!

'The spiral's end,' you hear yourself say.

ERMA

I stake out Sam Hell even though I suspect my dictaphone isn't in there and it isn't worth risking my life for anyhow. I tell myself I'm collecting data, conducting research until the police call me back. I want to have something substantial to tell them. And I feel it in my gut: there are answers over there in the basement.

I spy on Sam Hell at different times of the day and night and log observational data. I build up a picture of how the street looks across a twenty-four-hour period. I conduct an ethnography of this shit hole.

I spot trends.

Roberto Agrioli starts his day at the club every morning. Roberto arrives in a clapped-out car – a tan Holden Commodore, 766 VAL – and parks in a rear dock, taking the back entrance into the club. A woman – always the same woman – steps out at eight thirty and heads up to the McDonald's in the mall where she buys breakfast for him and brings it back. Every day, same routine.

The other men I saw in the club – the three guys dressed in black shirts who threw me out – they're the bouncers. I'm yet to see them all rostered on together but it probably happens on the weekends. Each weeknight thus far, one of them is on the door with one of the dancers helping out.

The club does a brisk trade. It's a downmarket crowd but not too tragic. Lots of single men, lots of older men. No couples. No groups. They turn away bucks parties and football teams. Sam Hell is on a steady course and trying to stay that way. Maintaining a low profile.

The only surprise is who I spot heading in there one bright Tuesday afternoon: Craig. He's in and out in about five minutes while the woman from the house – Carrie – double-parks in a bus zone out front. Neither of them look super excited to be running this particular errand. Craig almost makes me as they peel up Brunswick Street. His eyes catch mine. I duck into a side street. Wait a beat. Step back out and see the car idling at the lights.

I can read the number plate. I write it down.

They drive away.

The rest of the time, I try to appear normal, untroubled. I go to the Centre. Take lunch with Kanika and listen to her stories. She has a new boyfriend. He's an Althusser guy. Really laying it on: smokes a fucking pipe, tells her he hates his father. I don't give an opinion. I want to care, to help even, but everything sits behind a buffer I can't turn off. It's not a choice anymore.

At the gym, I'm strong and moving well. My wrists ache for an hour every morning but my cross is really coming along. One night in sparring, I catch one of the trainers with it and he laughs and says, 'Lady, you're getting fast.' It's true. I guess a near-death experience is good for something.

What it hasn't solved is my HR problem. The UQ unit overseeing my case starts calling me so often I have to answer. A man tells me that they've set a date for a 'hearing'. It's just another meeting but I need to come prepared to argue a defence. He reads out a bunch of instructions and policy numbers. A week from today, he says. I don't write any of it down. It's all pointless detail. Minutia.

It's Wednesday night. My apartment is abnormally quiet. I live beside a tall, eight-storey apartment block that over-shadows my building, and it's loud, even on a weeknight, and it's New Farm so there's always foot traffic as well. Wealthy neighbours taking a stroll after late dinners, students fresh off the bus, girls on smoke breaks from the halfway shelter down the road. There's always something going on. But not tonight. Tonight, it's so quiet that the quiet wakes me up.

My phone rings. The landline, in the living room.

I let it go.

Harlowe stands up on the end of the bed and watches the empty doorway.

The answering machine clicks in.

Archibald Moder's tinny voice echoes out:

—*isn't it? I think it really appealed to the young man in me. Role-playing games are quite open. A player can do a lot with*

138

their character, everything from naming them, writing their history, their backstory and so on, through to embodying their mannerisms during the game. I played with a woman once who insisted on playing men, affecting a gruff voice, sitting with her legs splayed and all of that sort of business. Have you ever played one of these games, Miss Wasserman?

It's not my sort of thing.

No other role-playing then? Somewhere else, perhaps?

No.

Hmmm. I think we all play roles, Miss Wasserman. It's what I could never understand about the eighties panic, all that media attention and so forth. All the moral arbiters were so scared of losing the youth to fantasy. But is it such a fantasy? To act as someone else? To pretend as a means to collaborate with others? To cope? Isn't that—

Beep.

I run to it, play it back. The audio quality is the same as last time. A recording of a recording. But this time someone is moving around on the call. Not Moder, not Jenny, this is someone else on the other end of the phone, holding a device. The recording phases in and out, louder and softer. On the line, I can hear someone snap the audio off before hanging up. A cold flush of blood flows down my neck and into my arms.

That's the fucking dictaphone.

4.03 a.m. Pre-dawn.

Panicking.

Screw it.

I call Detective Edwina at the police station and get some lackey instead. I rant into the receiver like a madwoman.

Five minutes later, Edwina calls me back. 'Wanna drop by the station?' she says, tired and bored. 'I'm rostered on.'

The Valley police station is an old stone building on the outskirts of the precinct. I wait in the foyer. This place looks like some relic from the colonies: the exact sort of thing every Aboriginal teenager dreads, no doubt. A couple of years back, the cops who worked out of this monument rounded up young black *troublemakers* and drove them out to the suburbs where they dumped them, sans shoes. It was a warning. The cops who did it are still on the job. They could be here this morning. That's Brisbane for you.

I wait on a bench. On the wall opposite there's a message board full of flyers. Most are Crime Stoppers bills but there's a large picture of a handgun sitting on some old paint tins and the title: 'Any Illegal Firearm Is a Terrible Crime Waiting to Happen'. Another reads, 'Be Security Smart This Weekend'.

Christ.

Good advice.

Along one edge of the message board, there's a column of 'Missing Persons' notices. Mostly men. A lot of young men. A wash of hard stares and bad hair. They all look four-fifths psychotic but there's one guy whose face looks uncannily familiar. Something I can't—

'Miss Bridges?'

A thin man in a uniform stands behind the counter. He waves me over to a side door. I get up and stand waiting beside it.

'Damn. Ya fit aren't ya, Miss Bridges?' says the cop behind the counter. 'Hey, Linda. Come look at this girl's arms.'

Another cop puts her head around. They both give me the once-over. I'm in my gym sweats.

'You ever think about becoming a cop, Miss Bridges?' says the policewoman.

'No. And it's Doctor Bridges, if we're going with the Oxford pleasantries.'

The door emits a harsh buzz.

'In you go,' says the policewoman.

I shove the door. It's heavy and opens with a loud click. There's a hallway behind it. Detective Edwina stands in a doorway halfway along. 'In here,' she says.

It's an open plan office. No privacy, but there's only one

other cop in here tonight. Edwina's desk is across the room and it's a pigsty. Towers of files and books, piles of food wrappers and half-empty water bottles, dozens of loose-leaf pages pinned to the cubicle walls. Half the desk is taken up with an ancient printer, a big boxy thing.

'I've been meaning to call you,' Edwina says. 'So, what's up?'

'Sure. I told the guy on the phone. Did they tell you?'

'Yeah, yeah, that's right. Something about a prank call. And you think, what?'

'I think it's related.'

'Related to what? The break-in at your place last year?'

Is that what they're calling it now?

I look at my hands. 'They're leaving recordings of her on my machine.'

'Who?'

'Jenny. The girl who shot me.'

'OK. So, tape recordings.'

'They're from the work Jenny was doing for me. She was interviewing people. Someone is calling me and playing the interview recordings down the line.'

'Are they threatening?'

'Yeah, it's scaring the shit out of me.'

'Right. But what's actually said? Do they threaten you personally?'

'Nothing's said. It's just a recording. I can play you one.'

'No, that's all right.'

'I brought it down with me.'

'No, it's fine. Look, I can't really do much until they threaten you. You don't have caller ID, I'm guessing?'

'It doesn't come up. There's some other stuff. I found out Jenny was stripping. She worked in a club up the road called Sam Hell. I think that's where she got the gun.'

Edwina purses her lips. 'But we've got the gun. And stripping's not illegal. You're not snooping around, are you? I told you not to do that. I told you that last time. I definitely told you that.'

'I know but that fucking . . . that recording they're playing is important to me. This can't be legal. It's harassment.'

'It's something,' says Edwina. 'It could be anyone. You have enemies at work? Friends of Jenny's? Does anyone know you're looking for this stuff?'

'Everyone knows I'm looking for it.'

An uncomfortable smile creeps across her face. 'There's not much I can do. Not yet. My advice is, go home and change your phone number and see if that works. I'm pretty sure it will. Now, is there anything else?'

'Jenny's boss, at the strip club. He's one of the Agriolis.'

Edwina runs her hands down her thighs. 'OK. And?'

'Well, that's important, right?'

'Not really. They own clubs all over the Valley. Listen, Erma, I know this is tough to hear but here's the thing. *We* have to move on as well. It's not just you. The fact that someone *might* have given your friend a gun isn't really new information. I can't do anything with that at the moment, OK?'

143

'You said you were going to look and see if any of Jenny's stuff was here. Did you do that at least?'

She stands up. 'I looked. There's nothing here. Let's get you out of here. Go home, change your number. See what happens.'

She takes me back to the hall and yells, 'Davie? Door.'

On the way out, I stop by the missing persons wall and look at the message board again. That one poster jumps out. The same guy.

Something about him.

A nondescript young white dude.

Blue eyes.

Short hair.

Could be one of a dozen of my students. Two dozen.

His poster reads, 'Police are appealing for public assistance to help locate missing man Andrew Michael Besnick. Mr Besnick, 20, is known to frequent St Lucia, West End and Fortitude Valley, and in July of 2004 he advised family that he was moving from Highgate Hill to New Farm. He has had no contact with his family since that time and was reported missing in September.'

St Lucia. That's the campus.

Student.

I inch closer. I glance around. The cops at the reception desk are hunched over, looking into a computer screen, eyes averted.

I rip the poster down.

Hit the doors.

It's cold out. An empty Wickham Street. Light on the horizon. A new morning.

We *have to move on.*

They don't want to deal with this.

Can't.

Won't.

It'd be nice to have choices.

In 1984, Bantam cashed in on the success of the Choose Your Own Adventure novels with a new series: Time Machine. There are two major differences. Firstly, Time Machine presents a type of YA historical fiction. You can travel back to the ice age, to the American Revolution, the Spanish Inquisition and so on. Second, in Time Machine the stories all have a fixed ending. One ending. The reader works to find this conclusion, encountering dead ends and correcting decisions along the way. It's interesting that branching narrative evolved *towards* something fixed, *towards* something closed and limiting, rather than the other way around.

As a kid, the Time Machine books were always my favourites. *Sail With the Pirates. Wild West Rider. Secret of the Knights.* I felt smarter having read them. And I loved the rules each book contained. Getting the reader through these books required a bit of scaffolding, hence the same four rules were outlined in the introduction to each book:

1. Don't kill anyone.
2. Don't change history.

3. Don't take anyone with you when you jump through time.
4. Follow the instructions.

Funny, as rules to live by – as an adult – they're not bad. You could do worse. But in a series completely fixated on course correction – all to get to that satisfying, singular conclusion – the reader absolutely has to break rule number two and *change history*. At least *your own history* anyway. You spend the whole book reversing your mistakes, which is a beautiful lie, isn't it? No wonder they sold so many copies.

This isn't even my main critique of the Time Machine books, or the genre as a whole. My main problem is that these books force an account of *you*. We're talking about fictional novels that, in a quiet, sneaky way, dominate you. These novels interpellate you. Do you want to correct your mistakes? Then be the hero these novels want you to be and don't deviate from the story.

You may be a secret agent.

An adolescent detective.

Young Indiana Jones (there are tie-ins).

A barbarian.

But your *interior* is always constructed by the author. None of these characters are written to account for any of your moods or any disposition other than the composed and rational self. *You* never freak out in these stories, even while under attack from vampires and lizard men and samurai. The heroic *you* at the centre is always so composed, so neat, so good and jolly and kind.

It's not real.

This is just a repeatable, idealised version of *you*.

You're always fine.

You don't lie to yourself.

You don't doubt.

You don't chew yourself up.

You don't hurt people.

You're the hero, after all.

You're up to this. You can handle it. *You* with your blank backstory and your designated role and your whole life reduced to binary sets of choices and do-overs.

If only.

I keep staking out Sam Hell. I find myself standing on Brunswick Street in the mouth of an alleyway with my fists clenched and rammed into my hoodie pockets, watching, waiting for something to happen. Voices bounce around in my head.

Have you ever played one of these games, Miss Wasserman?

It's not my sort of thing.

My whole body tenses when I hear the phone ring now.

Then on a Thursday afternoon at work, all hell breaks loose. I'm in my office, half-asleep at my desk, when the wall shudders hard enough to knock one of my degrees to the floor.

Kanika.

By the time I'm in the hall, Howard is running through her door. 'I'm fine,' she screams, followed by, 'I'm not bloody fine. Shit! Shit! Shit!' I can't see her but I can hear her crying.

A postgrad hangs back in the hall with me.

'What is it?' I say. 'What's happening?'

The postgrad's eyes widen. 'Didn't you see the email? They took another one.'

'What do you mean?'

'Someone grabbed a girl last night. Pulled her into a van down by the ferry terminal and drove off. Security just sent through a briefing.'

The door to Kanika's office slams shut. I go back to my desk and check my inbox. There's a photo and description of the missing girl. Sarah Holdings, nineteen, blonde, five foot eight. Tan/cream knit jumper, jeans, black backpack. She's a first-year undergrad studying history. The van she was pulled into is dark grey. It was parked on a road I jog along often.

So, it's bad.

Real bad.

Sarah Holdings kind of looks like me.

That night, Howard takes us all to the staff bar, telling Kanika there's nothing more they can do. They've already made all the calls: the Brisbane police, the Vice Chancellor, various women's groups on campus. The Centre has issued a press release: 'Enough's Enough: A Response to Our History of Violence'. We're all feeling a mix of things. Anger. Despair. Fear. Impotence. We drink the house red and slog through the bar's putrid bain-marie and try to keep it together.

At some point – later in the night – Kanika fishes the missing person flyer of Andrew Michael Besnick from my handbag. I've been using it as a bookmark. 'Why do you have this?' she says. 'Do you know him?'

I spin the stem of my wine glass between my fingers. 'I feel like I recognise him. I'm not good with faces but, I don't know, I've seen him.'

'It's Brisbane,' Howard says.

'True.'

'Have you looked him up?' says Howard.

'He's not on any of my class lists.'

Kanika refolds the flyer. 'It's odd, isn't it? I mean, it's weird that you're walking around with this but it's also odd that I spend all my time researching lost girls and never think about missing boys. We don't really have a lot of them, do we?'

'There were heaps of those at the police station. A message board full of them.'

'What police station?' says Howard.

'The Valley. I'm still looking for the dictaphone.'

'What dictaphone?'

'Did they have it?' says Kanika.

Howard's eyes are on me.

'Jenny's dictaphone. And no, they don't. They don't have any of her stuff. They're hopeless.'

Drunk and straight from the bar to the cab rank and then into the Valley alone. I sit on a bench in the student night scrum and watch Sam Hell across the street. I'm a stationary object in a heaving mass of tripped heels, bad hair and popped collars. It's so loud and insane that I forget myself for stretches.

At Sam Hell tonight, all three of the security guards I recognise are on duty. They stand around checking IDs and moving on the drunks and dickheads. This is the first time I've seen them all here together since that first morning with Roberto.

I change spots. I make my way into the little alleyway down the street where I can watch the club more intently from the shadows. There's a group of girls with me in the alley; they're standing guard while one of their crew vomits into a plastic bag. They don't seem to notice me and they provide a type of cover. I probably look like their frumpy sister.

3.13 a.m.

I pop a flu tablet from my bag and wait for it to spark me up. I rest my head against the alleyway wall.

My eyes close.

Just for a second.

Just for a moment.

Have you ever played one of these games, Miss Wasserman?
It's not my sort of thing.

A particularly loud groan from the alley jolts me awake. I head back out onto the street and into the throng. I hit the 7-Eleven for a coffee and take it around the block, down the perilous mall and along the back of the entertainment district until I come to the backstreets behind Sam Hell. Staying out of the light, I make my way to the rear loading dock. I haven't been back here for a day or two. It's usually empty but tonight it's full of cars. Two dark figures stand in the lot, smoking. I wait for them to finish and watch as they open the rear door of the club, light spilling out. It's Roberto Agrioli, out at night for a change. The other person is a woman. Thin, tall, old. Dressed in a long gown that hangs off her. An ex-dancer.

I creep over and start writing down licence plate numbers, car makes and colours. Up against the wall of the club, there's a little fenced-off car space covered in chain-link and shrouded under thick black gauze. This is where Roberto usually parks but tonight his tan Commodore is over by the kerb.

There's a hole in the gauze. I put my eye to it.

A new vehicle parked inside.

A grey van.

UQ St Lucia. A mid-afternoon dark sky. Another winter storm predicted. I take Campbell Road, jogging and watching the Forgan Smith tower track around in the distance. I overslept. My head is a cascading feed of data points. *Sarah Holdings, nineteen, blonde. Missing. A van down by the ferry terminal.* Jenny rode that same ferry to campus. We rode it together. I get instant flashes of it: *early evening, near dark. Jenny's hair sprayed across her face in the wind as the lights of the Story Bridge pass over. She tells me, 'I want to be like you, when I grow up.'*

I laugh and lean back into my seat. 'Who was that guy you were talking to tonight? The one with black hair?'

'Ryan? He's my room-mate. I think you're about to review the last part of his thesis.'

I shrug again, tipsy. 'I forget who is and isn't my student these days.'

'I like him,' Jenny says.

I'd forgotten that.

I keep jogging, pushing memories from my mind. I'm getting confused. I'm not sure I'm remembering things right, things I don't even want to think about. But that's the underlying trouble with memory. Memory isn't fact. Memory is subjective and loose. A memory can get close enough to fiction that the line blurs. What good is it?

I step up onto the front lawn of Forgan Smith without breaking stride. There are news trucks parked by the Centre steps, a cluster of them. Channel Nine, Seven, Ten. A group of technicians mill around. They have a small area at the Centre entrance lit for a broadcast. Cables snake out.

I show my staff card to a security guard nearby and he ushers me into the building. In the foyer, I find Howard, Kanika and two other researchers: Melissa Gregg from the cultural studies unit downstairs, and Roberta Binyon. Roberta steps close and puts an arm over my shoulder. I don't really know Roberta. Not well enough for this. All I know about Roberta is that she loves crying. She cries at every student event, every reading, every meeting. She might actually be studying crying. Lachrymology or something. True to form, she is crying today. 'It's just so sad,' she says and she shows me a photograph of a teenaged girl. Everyone else is holding a similar photo. They're the portraits from Kanika's office wall, the missing girls.

Howard spots me and says, 'There you are.'

'What is this?'

'We're doing a spot for TV.'

'OK.'

Kanika grabs me by the arm. 'You were supposed to be

here half an hour ago. I've emailed you four times. Go get changed.'

When it's time, we all stand in line before the cameras on the steps of Forgan Smith. Howard says a few words before introducing Kanika. We hold up our photographs as she makes her call to arms.

'Laura Hartop, Kelly Anson, Rosario Faust, Maya Kibby and Sarah Holdings. These are only five names from a possible fifteen. Five real people, real women, all taken. *This, must, stop.* These women were taken from us while the very institution that promises them a duty of care looks the other way. This is not a hoax. My data shows a very clear pattern of prolonged aggression from an unnamed perpetrator or perpetrators—' Roberta really starts bawling at this '—and if your daughter or sister or friend attends this facility for her education, then her life is now in clear danger. It's time for the University of Queensland and the Queensland Police to actively address the . . .'

The glare off the cameras casts the whole scene in an eerie golden light. *Is this happening?* The world slows. I look at the back of the photograph I'm holding. There's an inscription: 'Laurel Colegrave UQ Gatton, 1996'.

' . . . and so I say to you today, it *must* stop,' shouts Kanika. 'If we don't act now, as a community, I fear we will render this institution unsafe forever. Thank you.'

Voices roar. Cameras start flashing. *Pop. Pop. Pop.* We're supposed to rip our photographs in half now – that's the plan – but I freeze. I'm just holding mine, staring into Laurel Colegrave's blank face. I've never been to Gatton. I didn't know we had a campus out there.

Pop. Pop. Pop.

Kanika snatches the photo from me and tears it in half. 'This is nothing,' she screams for the cameras.

Pop. Pop. Pop.

A monstrous wind comes in, blasting us all back a step, the chill of winter rain in it. The TV people look to the sky. Another gust arrives. Then another volley of questions.

'Fuck this,' I whisper.

Roberta reels around and hisses, '*What did you just say?*'

The city is flash flooding by the time I reach New Farm. Thick torrents of water rush the gutters. I buy a flat white and head into the Coles, straight to the Health and Beauty aisle and to the vast rainbow of hair dye they stock there. The best thing about being blonde is that it's interchangeable. A clean canvas. I need something dark. My natural inclination is Jet Black but it's going to look terrible. My skin isn't what it should be, courtesy of my stakeout diet and the lack of sleep. Besides, black hair on paper white skin is strictly for teenage runaways. It's a beacon. *Please fuck with me.* Same thing with Intense Red, although I could probably pull that off. I just don't want that sort attention, so I play it safe and grab something called Espresso Brown.

Back in my apartment, I pull out the dress I wore to a

wedding three years ago – black, neat – and match it with woollen stockings. I dye my hair in the bathroom sink and do my makeup the way Dora used to do it.

We need to bring out those eyes, girl.

The whole thing starts to feel enchanted and eerie.

When I'm done, the long mirror in the bathroom shows me a picture of my long-lost sister. I look just like her. A well-kept woman.

Is this who I could have been?

I look like the sort of person who has a clearly defined office job and a successful partner, someone who can channel their ambition and stress into something useful, who can aim it directly at things. A couple of kids. A mortgage. A marriage. The right politics. A pleasant demeanour. A future. A decent handbag. Proper holidays. The whole deal.

Disguises always betray the wearer.

I stare into my eyes.

What else is in there?

Who else?

I've always found it upsetting how we can just recreate ourselves.

Back in the Valley.

Friday night.

Drunks slipping over in the rain.

A horrible vibe running like a cold streak.

I'm in my regular alleyway, pumping myself up for the

walk across the street to Sam Hell. I have two small pictures in my hand: Jenny Wasserman and Sarah Holdings. Two blondes. One possible connection: that door, right over there.

I start walking.

But my phone vibrates.

'Hello?'

'Erma, it's me.'

Dad.

I say, 'Is everything OK?'

'Oh, you know. Have you spoken to your mother lately?'

'No. Is she all right?'

'She is. I mean, I think she's fine. I just wanted to call because Euan was arrested last night.'

Dora's husband. Or ex-husband now. The guy hanging around our family house while my sister recuperated from that car crash all those years ago. They were together a long time. Euan's the reason we don't talk.

'I heard she left him?'

'I don't know. She doesn't talk to me about him.'

'What happened?'

'He hurt a woman,' my father says. 'It was some woman he worked with. I don't know much more but, your mother, you really should call her. Or you should try, at least.'

Should, should, should.

My breath turns thick.

My face burns.

'Thanks, Dad. I'll try and call.'

'How are you? I've been thinking . . .'

'Yes?'

He pauses.

I feel a blankness sweep the rest of it away.

'Dad, I'll call you back. I've got to go.'

I hang up.

It's not a sign, it's not an omen.

It's not useful data.

It's not relevant.

I recognise the security guard on the door but he doesn't recognise me in my new outfit. 'Half price for girls,' he says. Downstairs, after a slow descent in heels, I find the club almost empty. There's a lone dancer working the sad T-shaped stage. A small group of middle-aged men sit around the edge of it, gawking. Further back, another half-dozen men sit at tables, some accompanied by dancers, some alone. Stage light flickers on their stone faces like they're watching a screen. I'm still standing by the stairs, taking it all in, when a woman in a fluorescent green bikini wanders out of the gloom.

'Hey, darl.'

'Hi.'

'You need a drink?'

'Sure.'

Her body is toned to the point of muscle and bone. It's the sort of thing that probably looks great onstage but up close her tight biceps and calves give her a physical menace.

I order a gin and tonic and take a seat near the back of the club. On the sound system 'Drop It Like It's Hot' cuts sharply into 'In Da Club'. The girl onstage keeps grinding. The men sit around, motionless.

'Here we are.' The woman in the bikini places my drink on the little table beside me and swivels into an adjacent chair. She crosses her legs with exaggerated precision. 'Let me guess. First time in a place like this? You meeting someone?'

I smile. 'Yes and no.'

'You want a smoke? I'm technically on a break.'

'I'm good. What's your name?'

'Leia.'

'Like Princess Leia?'

'Never heard of her.' Leia blasts out a jet of smoke. 'I'm just fucking with you. Who are you?'

Despite all the dread running raw under my skin, there's something calming about Leia. She's that good at her job. I tell her my name is Samantha.

'OK, Sammy, at the end of this cigarette, you've gotta buy me a drink or I'm going back to work.'

'I'm actually looking for someone.'

'Another dancer?'

'Do you know a girl called Jenny? She worked here last year. Blonde. About my height. Big eyes.' I haven't even completely opened my hand to show her the photograph when she reaches over and closes my fist.

'You don't want to do that in here, darl. And I don't care.'

161

Leia gets up and walks away.

I head to the bathroom. I shut myself in a stall, take long deep breaths. *It's fine. This is all a mistake. Just get out of here.* I leave the stall and wash my hands alongside a plump girl touching up her make-up. I assume she's another dancer. She's wearing a pigtail wig and lederhosen.

I hold my photos up to the mirror. 'You seen either of these two?'

The dancer's pupils momentarily dart across. 'Maybe,' she says.

'I can pay you.'

'Why?'

'I'm a friend of theirs, their teacher, actually.'

'They runaways? They don't look like runaways.' She snaps her makeup kit shut.

'One of them used to work here.'

'I ain't seen either of them working here.'

I push open the door and step back out into the loud throb of the club. I'm standing a few feet from the bathroom door, taking in the stage show – a new girl, blonde, young, just like Jenny – when an arm wraps fast around my chest and another drags my feet up, sweeping me into the air. I'm so confused I don't scream, opting for, 'Hey!' before a sweaty palm tightens across my mouth.

We're off the main floor of the club before I can get a handle on the situation. There's two of them, two men. One on either end, carrying me like a dead body.

A bright spray of light washes over.

The club music mutes.

Parked cars in my perpendicular view.

We're behind the club in the lot where I saw the grey van last night.

I thrash around. The guy holding my legs reaches up and punches me in the stomach. I nearly puke into the hand covering my mouth. Tears roll sideways out of my eyes.

The door opens again.

The music blares.

Mutes.

The hand comes away from my mouth, and I swallow a scream. They stand me up in front of Roberto Agrioli. He's heavier-looking up close. A short stocky unit. He glances at me then turns and lights a cigarette. He stands there a few seconds and takes a drag while I wait. 'So,' he says, 'this is no good.'

'Look, I just—'

And I'm folded over on the ground before I know I've been punched again. It's an expert tap. Straight into the kidneys. I start to whimper.

Breathe into it. Breathe in—

'Yes? Yes, you understand now don' you, you dumb bitch? You're not allowed to interrupt me,' says Roberto. He squats down, trying to get my attention. 'Who the fuck are you? My boys say you've been hanging around the club like a bad smell all week. Now you've got everyone's panties in a bind. This is no good. No good at all. Who are you?'

I bring my legs in underneath me. 'I'm no one.'

'No, too late for that,' says Roberto. He puts his cigarette in the side of his mouth then drags my face in close to his. 'Nooooo!' He pads around his belt line and produces a six-inch knife. 'I *know* you, don't I? You came to see me not long ago.' He glances up at the bouncers and says, 'You two can go back inside. Don't let anyone out here.'

The other men leave.

I say, 'I'm just looking for my friend. That's all.'

'That's *not* all.' He points the tip of the blade towards me. 'This is not a good place for you to be putting your nose in where it's not wanted. Your friend, yes? The blonde one. She was a busybody too. Now I want you to lift your dress up for me.'

'What?'

'You heard me. Do it slow.'

He brings the knife right over to my face, his arm fully extended. In Muay Thai, you never really see a knife waved around like this. You don't show a weapon before you use it. It's a mistake.

I slip my heels off. 'No. I'm not doing that. I have money.'

Roberto frowns. He takes the cigarette from his mouth and flicks it away. As he does, his knife hand shakes and I go for it. I get right into his space, pushing my left forearm into his wrist and wiping the blade away. I ram the other hand – palm open – up under his chin.

It works. Roberto's head snaps back.

From there, I punch down into the elbow of his knife arm, folding it up and bringing it under my armpit as I turn into him. There's a sickly crunch as the whole limb comes out of its socket. Roberto squeals like he's never been hurt before.

The blade falls to the ground. I don't bother picking it up.

As I'm standing there, holding him, trying to take a second, Roberto surprises me with a half-assed lunge for my throat. I turn my head, sweep his hand away and step around to the side, my elbow locking around his neck. Then I kick his left knee out and slam him into the ground. Winded, he's so open and dazed that my first three blows connect without much defence on his part. He starts to moan, losing consciousness already.

I pause.

Roberto starts to drag himself away. We're between two parked cars now. I kick him twice to stop him moving. Then I turn him back over and get on top of him to work on him some more. My fists drive into his old skin, into his weak face, his mouth. I pummel his body to bring his arms down, then go back to the head, working him back and forth. At some point, I realise I'm screaming. Oblivious. My hands dripping with blood.

Despite the winter cool, I sweat through my clothes, tossing and turning in my bed, dark visions roaring through the room.

Roberto struggling.

Roberto's eyes.

Desperate for comfort, I slide a hand between my legs. I'm already wet.

The heat of him.

Was it just? Was it fair?

Is he dead?

The orgasm surges up.

There's a lot of fighting in the books I study. One of the lead series is called Fighting Fantasy, but that's just one example. All the gamebooks within the broader subgenre have their own 'fight mechanics' or combat systems. These systems vary but they always revolve around tactical decision making and dice play. Within the communities of readers who love these things, combat is a major point of discussion. The fighting, it seems, is the main attraction.

At times, the combat systems have produced notorious

examples of unfairness, the most famous of which is in a book called *The Crimson Tide*. In that book, you take the role of a young child – that's the main character – and very early in the adventure you confront a giant mud worm with a fighting skill-level far exceeding your own. There's no way to defeat the worm except via improbable luck with the dice. No tactic will save you. You're just a kid, after all. Enough people have found themselves dead at the hands of this worm – in the first act of the story – that readers started asking the author Paul Mason about it at conferences and meet-ups. *What were you thinking there, Paul? Do you love dead children? Is it a metaphor? Is the book an abuse narrative?* Eventually, Mason admitted what a lot of people suspected: it was a typo. You weren't supposed to die like that. It was supposed to be fair. But another kind of luck – unrelated to the dice – intervened. Over time, I've come to see *The Crimson Tide* as an accidental truth. Unlike linear first-person fiction, you *can* die in a gamebook. But in an unfair gamebook, death lurks in random, stupid, unjust corners, just like real life.

As if on cue, the landline in the living room starts ringing.

8.13 a.m.

I'm too scared to pick it up.

The answering machine clicks in.

Archibald Moder's precise therapy-patter echoes down the hall to my room. I put a pillow over my face and scream. It's still going on when I snap out of it.

167

—and if you find that amenable I feel—
Something different this time.
I get up and walk towards the phone.
—just call my assistant and he'll set it up for you. I'm sorry it's taken so long to return your calls. I don't take on a lot of interview requests these days but as long as this won't waste a whole day, I'm happy to have you out to the house. My assistant's mobile number is oh four, three seven one, nine, double—
'Holy shit.'
I play it again.
It's not the dictaphone recording.
It's not a prank call.
Moder wants to resit the interview.
I crawl back into bed and lie there.
This is a second chance.
And in my mind, *a reward*.
I close my eyes.

SERO

18

Through the darkness comes amber and bronze. Walls, a window, curtains. The sound of human movement. Muted voices floating up underneath you.

This is the inn.

You sit up from the bed and pat your chest, expecting the skin there to be charcoaled from the priest's beam of light. Nothing. You experience stabs of recall:

Rohank's voice in your mind.

The strobing room.

Heat. Sand. Wind.

Dark water.

A dream?

A bright pathway lights up your synapses. A desire. With absolute certainty you know the way forward, the way to regain your memories.

You need to follow Rohank's vision.

You need to ride into the desert.

19

They call the long flatlands beyond the city a desert but

it features no dunes or pits of sand. Instead, it is a giant shallow basin of red dirt, some monstrous crater in the earth surrounded by mountain ranges. The thing looks about a week's ride in diameter but you know, in your heart, that the site you're looking for – the site Rohank showed you – is two days west, a straight line between the morning sun and Rohank's tower on the edge of the city behind you.

The horse senses your resolve and performs with an unprecedented level of cooperation. It breathes heavily, sucking hot air into its lungs as it gallops. *It's out there.*

20

Night falls and the sun is replaced by a moon so bright the landscape stays visible. You make camp as best you can: unroll a blanket on the flat sand, lie close to the horse for shelter.

Sleep comes quickly until something takes hold of your ankle. It keeps hold as you try to snatch your leg up, still dazed. The force of the recoil pulls a skeletal arm up out of the desert floor. A wretched torso follows, a body of moving bones crawling out of the ground towards you. Another arm erupts from the sand by your left shoulder: a hand reaching out, a mess of rotting bones entwined with a tight weave of white sinew.

Demons.

The horse brays and stands, on the verge of bolting.

Sword, sword, sword . . .

You kick at the skeletal figure at your feet, loosening its grip before rolling and unsheathing your weapon, springing up into a fighting stance. The sand around you is alive with horror now. Faces and torsos and arms swim and squirm. Another hand circles your ankle. You reach down and drag a beast up out of the ground and hack away at it with the sword. Once sawn in two, it falls back into the maelstrom. You see it clearly for a moment: human bones made alive by desert snakes. A monstrous pale whipping beast operates the spine with the serpent's head pouring out the mouth of the skull.

The horse twists and bucks. You scramble up into the saddle as it rears and begins to run. Together, you make for dawn on the horizon.

This land is possessed.

No escape.

Destination or death.

The end of it, surely.

ERMA

I sleep through an entire day and feel no better for it. I ache from heel to wrist. My hands are swollen, knuckles torn open. Around three o'clock, I return the call to Archibald Moder. His assistant picks up. He tells me his name is Harlan and he gives me an address right out on the back roads, about two hours south of the city. I look it up: it's the mountain country down near the border. 'If you get lost, call us,' Harlan says. He sounds young, with some of Moder's vocal mannerisms. A son or nephew, perhaps. Harlan tells me they still need a few days to clear a block of time in the old man's schedule. 'He's frail but still quite active, unfortunately.'

'That's more than fine. I'll come out as soon as he can see me.'

It's cold in the apartment. I shuffle around with a quilt for a cloak, unable to do much more than boil the jug and order pizza. Then, hunched over in the afternoon dusk listening to Radio National, it finally dawns on me that I might have killed a man. I really put Roberto down last night. He's middle-aged, out of shape. He might not survive a beating like the one I gave him. But it doesn't seem so sinister, if I'm honest. It feels like a dream. Or like a memory, something misremembered. I don't feel like a villain. The truth is, I don't feel anything.

A week later and the Centre for Creative Writing and Cultural Understanding is unusually busy. Our TV appearance unleashed all this. Postgrads and research assistants mill around. A cloth banner is being painted in the foyer. The photocopier runs hot spitting out posters demanding 'The Time Is Now for Campus Safety'. Howard takes his usual student consults down the hall but even the serial non-attenders are in today. In the Squadroom next door, Kanika's phone is ringing off the hook. I can hear her talking through the wall.

I'm trying to tune it out. I'm deep in my research for the Moder interview. It's set for tomorrow. Mid-morning. In the days since I spoke to Harlan, all I've done is sit around the apartment preparing. I've reviewed every clipping there is. I've revised my already bulging files. I've even replayed most of his novels, taking notes and dog-earing pages. My interview with Moder is going to sound effortless and casual, but underneath I'll be probing. I'm going to the heart of it with him. It's no small thing to interview a former psychoanalyst. I've read enough failed attempts. I've listened to him reduce journalists to tears in archival recordings. Age has softened him apparently, but, even still, he won't be an easy nut to crack.

I'm focused on the research because there's also a bunch of other noise in my life I'm trying to blot out.

I'm not sleeping again. I spend every night waiting for the Agriolis or the cops to walk through the front door. And, two days ago, I dodged another barrage of calls from human resources. They've set an agenda now, another interview, something to discuss 'the preliminary findings of an internal investigation concerning personal conduct allegations made in 2004 by a former research assistant'. That last part reads like an administrative oversight. I guess the cat is out of the bag now.

Jenny.

More Jenny.

Fucking me from the grave.

That little—

'Erma?'

Kanika stands in my office doorway.

'Yeah? What's up?'

'They found her. They found Sarah Holdings.' Kanika hands me a piece of paper, a printout from the *Courier Mail* website. My eyes hit a familiar name in the first paragraph and it's like a knife sliding into my skull:

BRISBANE STUDENT FOUND DEAD IN
HOUSE OF MISSING MANSFIELD MAN
Police have discovered the body of missing University of Queensland student Sarah Holdings, 19, in the house of another missing person: Mansfield man Roberto Agrioli.

A crime scene has been declared, with Brisbane detectives and Scenes of Crime officers currently at the house. The investigation is . . .

I'm skimming down the page.

The Agrioli man, 46, was last seen at the Sam Hell night-club in Fortitude Valley between 3 and 4 a.m. . . .

Police believe Agrioli is a part-owner of the establishment and may have been assaulted immediately prior to his disappearance. He is wanted for questioning in relation to Holdings' death.

Holdings has been missing since . . .

I pretend to read the rest but I'm stalling. I trawl back to anything I might have said to Kanika about Agrioli or Sam Hell or my ad hoc surveillance operation down in the Valley.

I cough. 'Well, there's something to be said for . . .' and I look up.

Kanika's pale. She's holding on to my shoulder, steadying herself.

'Are you OK?'

'I've got to find a new research focus,' she says. She has no idea what's going on with me. She's completely dazed. 'I . . . I can't do this anymore. *This* day in and out? What was I thinking? I need to change my life.'

And I'm listening but her voice is a whisper in my ear,

drowned out by a sensation much, much louder. A big emotion flowing through, flooding me, making the office cramped and oppressive. My mind is so clouded that it takes a moment to realise what it is.

It's relief.

If Roberto killed Sarah Holdings, Roberto might have killed all these other missing women too. All our disappearing students.

Is he the guy? Is he the killer?

And Jenny's right there in his orbit.

Was Jenny his accomplice? His victim?

Either way, Roberto got what was coming to him. No one will doubt my story if I have to tell it now. He came at me in the car park. I fought back. Even if I killed him with my own hands and his mafia friends buried him in a back lot somewhere . . .

I'm going to be OK.

No one cares about Roberto.

No one.

And maybe, just maybe . . .

I've accidently finished this thing.

Solved the mystery.

Case closed.

Kanika is gently holding on to my shoulder.

Archibald Moder's people insist on an ungodly 8.30 a.m. interview ('His morning brunch, Dr Bridges') and I've timed the journey out there at a little over two hours. I take the Story Bridge – still lit at this time of morning – and merge onto the highway, driving a drudgerous outbound commute through the city's suburbs, most of which reside behind corridors of sound abatement walls and real estate billboards. I refuel in Logan and wolf down a McDonald's breakfast over the *Courier*, noting the Agrioli case has dropped from page one to page four, then hit the road, driving around the arse-end of Beenleigh and into the winding roads that will take me to the mountains.

By eight o'clock, a muted sun sits in the grey sky overhead and I'm driving through misty forest corridors that absolutely no one associates with humid Queensland. These are the hinterland green spaces, the hills, once the original country of Brisbane's white trash but now home to the city's millionaire retirees and art patrons.

Up on the mountain proper, I drive through streets lined with two-storey timber colonials (all white), green hedges and gravel drives. I see yards with fountains and tennis

courts and decorative pools. The Moder property sits right
on the southern edge of Tamborine Mountain at the end
of a road branching out like a spire. To get there, I pass
through a long tunnel – an impossibly dark tree canopy
– to a small cul-de-sac at the end. There are two gates.
The right-hand one bears a small rusted emblem.

I leave the car idling and take a closer look at the
emblem, certain it can't be real. It is. An ornate shield
locked inside a cube-shaped spiral. The Zone Mover
logo. It's on the cover of every Archibald Moder book.
There's an intercom by the gate but I've been told to
call instead.

A familiar voice answers. The man himself. Moder laughs
a croaking, wheezing laugh and tells me to come on up.

Inside the compound, a wide concreted drive sweeps up
an incline to a house hidden in the treeline. A short way
along the drive, I come across a man standing in the centre
of the path. He's my age or a little older, and he's just
standing there, dressed in a tan polo shirt, cardigan and
tailored blue shorts. As I approach, I see that he resembles
a young Archibald.

The man comes to the driver's side window. 'Doctor
Bridges?'

'That's me. Are you Harlan?'

'I am. You can park over that way, just take that left-
hand path up there into one of the spaces. I'll take you
the rest of the way. There's parking up at the house but

none of it's covered and they're predicting hail.' Harlan points up at a circling green bank of cloud.

My designated parking space is in front of a large aluminium shed about the size of a regular house. A series of roller doors line the shed, facing the drive. I'm waiting by these doors when Harlan arrives on a motorised golf cart.

'Archie can't drive anymore but he won't let us sell the cars,' he says, motioning to the shed.

'How many does he have?'

'Too many. For someone who doesn't travel far, he's pretty keen on cars. There's one for every day of the week and two for Sunday.' He looks at my banged-up sedan. 'What's that? A ninety-eight Corolla? A ninety-nine?'

'I don't know.'

'You know, one of the groundsmen is due to service our fleet today. I could get him to give yours a look, if you're interested? We wouldn't want you breaking down in the rain on the way back.'

'It's OK.'

'You sure?'

'Yeah, yeah. It'll be fine. It got me out here.'

'OK then,' and Harlan revs the golf cart. 'Hop aboard.'

Up on the hill, the Moder residence is more modern than expected. The talk is that Archibald has lived up on the mountain for years but the house Harlan is driving towards is less than a decade old. It's a strange building: a three-storey A-frame, long across the roof like a scalene triangle. The walls are a mix of brushed steel and stone-work with large eaveless windows. The lights are on inside and, as the cart rounds the building, I can see people in there. A woman stands in the kitchen; another (shorter, in a white tracksuit) vacuums a side room. In the corner of an upstairs bedroom, two men stand at the window, surveying the gardens: one of these men is a doctor – a stethoscope lays draped over his shoulder – the other is much younger, with brown hair, wearing the same tan polo as Harlan.

'We have a few guests today,' Harlan says. 'Thus the early appointment.' He swings hard on the steering wheel, bringing the cart down a corridor lined with ferns. 'Here we are.'

I follow him through a door and upstairs. As we arrive at this second floor, he says, 'Do you need the bathroom?'

I tell him I do. I need to go but, more importantly, I need an unobserved moment to get my dictaphone recording. I've brought two with me. One to show Archibald – should he agree to be recorded – the other running on the downlow just in case. I didn't come all this way to walk away empty handed.

Stepping out of the bathroom, I glance down the hallway, wondering about the doctor and the young man. *Is Moder sick?*

Harlan reappears. 'You ready?'

'Ready as I'll ever be.'

He takes me to a wide-open room with views of the

tapering mountainside. In one corner, there's a plush-looking set of lounges and, reclining on one of them, I can see a silhouetted figure.

'You OK over there, Archie?' says Harlan. 'You want the lights on?'

'No, no.'

The figure waves a hand.

Come.

Harlan smiles and points a little bow in Archibald's direction as he backs out.

I don't feel nervous until I hold my arm out to take Moder's hand and see that I'm shaking. Seeing Moder up close, I'm flushed with recognition. He's remarkably well preserved for seventy-odd. Still a thin man but not frail. Still bald but clear skinned and soft-looking. While his face has sagged a little, it's hard to notice past the dark fixed eyes. The only surprise is the small silver earrings he wears, one in each ear. Other than that, he is still the handsome man of his author portraits. The man, I suddenly remember, my sister planned to marry. Dora's first crush.

'Good morning,' he says. 'It's Erma, yes? I hope the drive wasn't too much for you.'

'Not at all. This is a beautiful house, Mr Moder. Thanks for inviting me up.'

'Mr Moder is my father, god forbid. Everyone calls me Archie, dear. Now, sit down, sit. Do you need anything? I have coffee but I can call down for water or tea?'

'Coffee's good.'

There is a pot on the table between us. I watch him pour it out. Unlike me, his hands are steady.

'How long have you lived here, Archie?'

'Oh a few years now. Yes, a few years.'

We both stare out the window a moment. The mist has turned and rain silently sleets down. In the distance, I can see someone hurriedly pushing a wheelchair along a path by a grove of trees.

'My neighbour has a clinic up here,' says Archibald. 'They use the grounds. My guests find it odd but I've grown quite used to it. It's nice to have people around, even if they are the sick and frail of mind.'

'And you practised too, didn't you?'

'Oh yes. Psychotherapy. I had my own clinic right up until the fifth or sixth book, and even then I still saw the occasional client. A lot of authors dream of going full-time with their writing but I was the other way round. I found it hard to shake off my old life, even when the money became hard to argue with.'

I blurt out, 'I feel like I've so much to talk to you about.'

'I'm surprised people still care, to be honest. Especially someone such as yourself.'

'Oh no. I grew up with your books. I *loved* them. They meant so much to me. I remember when my sister and I found out you were Australian, it was in the paper, we couldn't believe it. It was such a big deal in our house.'

'Oh, thank you. It's been quite a long time now, Erma. Quite a long time, but I still get letters about the books, you know. No one really remembers me as their therapist, and I was a good therapist, but with the books, people still seek me out. It's very strange to think, ha, well, the books *were* my career in the end. But then, they were also only a small part of my life on the whole. There was so much more. Family, travel, work, other writing and what have you. Still, I'm very flattered people continue to read me. I was always very proud of whatever success I had with writing. Very proud. It was bloody better than people said it was, back in the day.'

'Archie, would you mind if I recorded our conversation? I should have already turned this thing on.'

'Oh, be my guest. The other one did.'

I put the dictaphone on the table. 'Yes, well—'

'What happened to her? She was a funny girl. Lovely to look at, but something . . . something strange about her too.'

'She died, actually. Suicide. It's very sad. Didn't Harlan pass that on? That's why I'm here. She died without handing over the interview.'

'Oh, I see. Harlan never tells me anything bad. They coddle me too much, *way* too much. I'm always telling them that.'

There's a pause. Moder stirs his coffee.

'OK. First question. I want to hear how you got started with gamebooks. Did you read the British stuff, or did you come to it from Dungeons & Dragons? How did it start?'

'My wife,' Archibald says. 'My wife was the one. She discovered role-playing. She was the one who put the idea in my head.' Sadie Moder is dead. She died in the eighties. No one knows how exactly. I don't have a single photo of her. 'She liked to play games, Sadie. It was something she inherited from her upbringing. She was quite poor, you know. Famously poor, in fact. A Wilson before she married me. My mother used to describe things as "even too cheap for the Wilsons", that sort of thing.'

'And she discovered Dungeons & Dragons? Or was there something earlier than that like Chainmail?'

'I can't rightly remember. She liked to dress up. That was part of it. But she was always very interested in fantasy and she loved dragons and Tolkien and that sort of thing. Dungeons too. And monsters, magic. The occult. Always very interested in the dark side of fantasy, my wife. She was a very unusual woman, a wild red-headed beauty. I loved her dearly. We were happy together. We had to work at it, as one does, but my marriage was one of the better ones. Are you married?'

'Me? God no.' I force myself to smile. 'So you wrote the first Zone Mover book for your wife?'

'That's right, yes. For her and Rebecca, our daughter.'

'I didn't know you had a daughter.'

'Oh yes. Children are a blessing. Rebecca is gone now too but you've met my son.'

'Harlan?'

'That's right. What else is on that list of yours?'

Over the next half-hour, Archibald Moder stares out the window and, almost unprompted, gives me the answers to my first five questions in long steady declarations. He's obviously ready to talk. Rehearsed even. He tells me about his debut, *The Rock Mines of Basida*, and the path he took to create the gaming system (a derivation of *The Forest of Doom*, a first edition mailed over from the UK by an uncle) and how his debut was submitted and edited.

'Yes,' he says. 'I wrote the early books for young people. They were the people buying the damned things, and besides, I quite like young people. It was only later on, once I'd made my money, that I started writing whatever I pleased.'

'And when was that? I've always thought of *The Unknown Warrior* as your first book for adults.'

'That's where I'd peg it too. That was eighty-seven. A big year.' He averts his eyes. 'I lost my wife that year.'

'How?'

'She committed suicide, like your friend. It was . . . it was a terrible business. My wife was quite ill. Mentally ill. No one could save her. No one. I'm sure of that.'

No one knows this.

'How do you feel about *The Unknown Warrior* now?'

'Oh, it has its problems but it's still a favourite. Probably my overall favourite, if I had to pick. The main character, as you probably know, is my only reappearing creation. I was quite obsessed with the barbarian for a while. I figure you know who I'm talking about. Sero the barbarian? Sero is the only thing that got me through those difficult times. It's funny to think of someone I made up as a close friend, especially someone so . . . so vacant. I mean what *is there* to know about Sero? We don't even know what gender Sero is, after all.'

'Did you leave that deliberately open?'

'Oh yes. Sero doesn't belong to any of us. Sero is everywhere.'

'It wasn't a pitch to female readers?'

'That too.'

I take a punt. 'Did your daughter like the character?'

'I'd lost her too, by then.'

'I'm sorry.'

'This is life, Erma. People come and people go. That's the hard part of getting older. You've got to live with other people's choices.'

'Sorry. What does Sero mean to you?'

He laughs. 'Have a guess. You should have worked it out by now, you're the scholar. No, better yet, what does Sero mean to you? Tell me that. Indulge an old man.'

'Chaos, regret . . . I move around with it. I can't pin that character down, even for myself. It's weird, I've been dreaming about Sero lately. Your turn.'

He laughs again. 'I don't know. I just wrote the thing. I can tell you this, Sero is where I put my, well, my violence, my anger. For me, that character is the zero, the base level. It's in all of us, don't you think? It was certainly in me after what happened with Sadie and Rebecca. To lose one's daughter, then one's wife. I wrote those books to contain myself, to capture all of that trouble, to put it some place safe. It all went into Sero. You have to put it some place, Erma. You really have to, if you want to survive.'

We break for morning tea under a rear awning. Wafer biscuits with cut fruit. Harlan appears briefly. Archibald's next appointment is running late so we have a little more time together. 'Good,' says the old man. With Harlan back out of sight, Archibald lights a cigarette and blows the smoke out into the grey rain. He takes a sip from his coffee and says, 'My GP told me I should quit smoking and that I should quit coffee. I told him, I might quit smoking one day, in my old age.' He winks at me. 'But I'll never give up coffee. I think I'd rather die.'

On the way back upstairs, we pass a closed room on the second floor that emits a soft electronic bleeping. A 'Do Not Disturb' sign hangs on the door, and above that there's a list of emergency phone numbers. Archibald walks past the room without comment but as he moves slowly along I have time enough to hear the gentle wheeze of a respirator inside.

As we drill down into the second half of Archibald's career, he starts to ask me more questions in return. I get what I need for my book – and it's more than anyone else before me – but a strange mood settles over the conversation, a refocusing of sorts.

Archibald taps the armrest of his chair and asks nervously, 'Do you write?'

'Only textbooks. Boring textbooks.'

'Pity. All writing takes is a sustained interest. Patience, I guess. You can learn the rest of it. If you've written a textbook, you're all set.'

'Maybe. I want to ask you about the period after the series ended. Have you written anything since *River of Dying*?'

'No, that was the last one. The end of the gold rush. Over the years, I've pecked away at things but it never amounted to much.'

'Was it writer's block?' I figure it's best to get this over with.

Archibald thinks. 'Not really. Do you have trouble with that?'

'No. What I do is technical. Would you say you decided to give up writing?'

'I guess so.'

'Why?'

'I'm not sure. Why does one start or finish anything?'

'Did something happen?'

'No, no. I just . . . I suppose I found other things to occupy my time, you see. I got sick of writing the series long before they cancelled it. There are only so many questions you can ask the reader after a time. There are only so many branches you can make. It gets repetitive.'

'What do you mean?'

'As the author of these kinds of things, you're constantly called upon to create all the scenarios where the reader can choose one thing or another. But there's not much to it. Right or left. Fight or flight. Go to this place or follow that path. Et cetera, et cetera. That's the part of it I didn't want to do anymore. I got sick of providing options.'

'But they're not *really* options, are they? I mean, you're still in control of the story.'

'Oh yes, absolutely. I guess I got tired of pretending. Isn't that odd. I've never told a woman that before.'

I don't know what he means by this.

'I didn't tell the other girl any of this,' he adds, as if this explains things. 'Her name was Jenny, yes?'

'That's right.'

'I think she was more interested in herself than anything I had to say. Which is fair enough, I guess. Young people can be like that.'

'I . . . ahhh—'

'You know, she told me some things about you. I should say she was more interested in you than herself. I should clarify that. Do you want to know the real reason I agreed to sit down with you this morning?'

'Uhm, sure.'

'She told me you slept with her boyfriend. All her boyfriends in fact, one after the other. She told me that. Isn't that an odd thing to tell someone like me, a stranger? She told me a lot of things, actually. She had a lot of . . . well . . .'

'What?'

'Anger.'

'And she told *you* this?'

'She told Andrew the whole story. Or maybe it was one of the others. She stayed for a couple of days. Did you know that? Oh, I thought she might have said.'

I don't know who Andrew is but I'm flustered by all this. I blurt out, 'What did she say about me exactly?'

'She told me that every time she met someone, her boss ended up hitting on them. That you were borderline pathological—'

'That's not—'

'She painted you as some sort of villainess. She said you threatened her, to make her come up here. Roughed her up. I was intrigued to meet this so-called monster, I have to admit.'

'Look, Archie, that's a load of nonsense. Jenny was . . . She had a lot of problems.'

'Oh, I'm sure, I'm sure. It was only when I saw you on the television that I even remembered all this. It was on the news the other week. You and your friends holding up those pictures of all those missing girls from the university. Terrible business that. But I saw your name on the screen and I thought to myself, I know that girl, she doesn't look anything like a monster to me.'

'I'm sorry you had to deal with Jenny bothering you. I really am.'

'It's fine. I think coming up here did her a lot of good in the end. She needed a break, I guess.'

'How many people live here? I saw a younger guy on the way in. For some reason, I thought he might be a grandson or a nephew or something.'

'No that's probably Andrew. He's a friend of Harlan's. He's been living here of late. Harlan gets lonely from time to time. He likes to have people around more than I do, which is fair enough. He was a student too, you know.'

Andrew.

Andrew and Harlan.

There's something there, right back in the outer reaches of my mind.

Archibald leans forward. 'Jenny told me you have a sister in Melbourne?'

'What? Ah, yeah. Just the one. She's younger. Dora.'

'How much younger?'

'Oh, not even a year. We're like twins.'

'Twins?'

'Virtually. Less than a year apart. It's a weird situation.'

'How so?'

I don't know where to take this. I shrug.

'Are you close to your parents?' he says.

'Ah, I—'

'Are you close to your mother?'

I shrug again. It's all I want to say.

Archibald seems oddly satisfied with my non-answers. 'Yes, yes. Families, they can be a source of such joy and such terrible agony. The problem with them is that they know you too well. You can't lie to your blood, Erma.

They see through it, see through everything. They see it all eventually.' Archibald looks past me. 'Is it time?'

I swivel in my chair and find Harlan standing there like a silent butler, his hands clasped together over the waistline of his shorts.

'Sorry to sneak up on you, Doctor Bridges. And yes, Archie, the man is here so you'll have to wrap this up.'

I stand up and straighten my skirt. 'Well, thank you both so much for your . . .' And I stop because Archibald has picked up my dictaphone. He is staring at it, turning it over in his hands.

'Dear, how do I turn this thing off?' he says.

I take a step towards him.

'It's small, isn't it?' he says. 'Are they fragile?'

'They can be.'

He holds the dictaphone out and as I take it from him – as my hand covers his and we're both holding the device – I see the slightest glimmer of a smile cross his face. It's more in his eyes than his mouth but it's there, precise and clear. 'Nice to meet you, Doctor Erma,' he says. 'Maybe we can chat more at some point. I think we could learn a lot from each other.'

'Yes. I'd like that. Thank you.'

'This way,' says Harlan.

I follow without looking back.

We take the hallway, the stairs, the corridor.

We ride the golf cart.

What is happening?

My heart pounds.

It ended weird.

Why did it end weird?

Harlan doesn't speak as we motor along. He brings the cart close to the bumper of my car then puts it in reverse, steering back towards the giant shed beside the car park. The bay door is open wide.

'What are we doing?'

'Oh, I'll show you his cars.'

'I really need to—'

'Two minutes. You'll love it,' he says.

He backs the cart into the shed and as we come in I see the doctor from the house. He's standing there in the open with another man beside him. Someone new. Behind them are a row of vintage cars.

'Hey,' says a voice behind me. 'Erma? It's me, Drew.'

A kid in glasses appears and walks towards the cart. He's smiling. 'We met at that pub that night with that cunt's sister.'

The world goes black, cloth material stretched over my face. I bring my hands up, and I'm screaming, lashing out. I grab a handful of someone's hair and a man grunts but then there's a crushing, choking arm around my throat.

Then a cold, sharp sting in my arm.

Then nothing.

PART THREE

SERO

21

A day's ride through the desert and the sky is washed in red and orange. The horse runs without pause, sensing something in the strange weather. You both sense the closeness of death. You are both afraid.

A hill appears in the distance, a mound in the desert floor.

'That way,' you tell the horse.

There's a cavern dug into one side of the mound, an opening the width of ten men and the height of two. A portal down. You recognise this place from Rohank's vision.

You dismount and lead the horse down. In the low light, there is a chamber of sorts. In the chamber there is a well and, behind it, a set of three doors dug into the earth wall. The horse pulls you to the well. You draw water and it looks clear and smells clean but you give it to the horse first.

The horse snouts around in the bucket but doesn't drink.

'Is it poison?'

The horse looks at you, then makes up its mind and starts lapping at it.

You fill your flask and say, 'I'll wait and see if you die first.'

While you wait, you inspect the doorways in the earth wall. Each has a jagged timber door. All unlocked.

The horse lets out a loud snorting neigh. He shakes his mane and backs up out of the cavern onto the desert floor above. There, the beast rises up on hind legs and neighs again.

Not poison, then.

'You look OK to me,' you say.

The horse snorts and shakes its head.

'You need to wait for me while I venture down into this horrible pit. Come back down. I'll tie you.'

The horse bolts.

No.

You clamber up the incline but there's no catching it. The beast has made its decision.

You're alone again.

22

You return to the three doors in the chamber and search your memory for Rohank's vision, asking for some hint or direction.

Heat.

Sand.

Wind.

Flying over a desert and into the night and down into dark blood-red sand and through it into a passage . . .

There was water too.

Dark water.

You drink from your flask, guzzling down every drop of the cool liquid. It tastes like rain. Not a grain of salt in it. A few flasks later, you investigate the doors further. Behind each is a pitch-black corridor. You cautiously throw stones down these corridors, checking their depth. All the stones disappear. You check the walls by the doors and as your eyes scan around you uncover crude symbols etched in the ceiling above each entranceway.

An arrow.

A cross.

A spiral.

Three doors and three symbols.

Exhausted, you curse the symbols, shaking your fist at them. Night is fast approaching. Those creatures will return if you stay out in the open. It's time to act.

'Show me,' you whisper. 'Show me.'

Without warning, a quiet voice in your mind returns the call.

If Sero takes the door marked with the arrow, turn to **23**. If it's the cross, turn to **24**. If it's the door marked with the spiral, turn to **25**.

23

Even with the door left open, the darkness envelops you quickly. The corridor is narrow. You follow the wall with one hand as a guide. With the other, you hold your sword at the ready, inching forward. You remember the nun who led you to your encounter with Rohank. You curse yourself for not bringing along a portion of her red crystal. A taste of that would help with this.

Time passes. You feel your bearings start to slip.

How far have I come?

Two hundred paces?

Two thousand?

You rest a moment on the earth floor. It's so quiet you can hear your heart beating. Without movement, the corridor seems to slip away. Minutes or hours pass in the void.

Then:

A bright flash of gold ignites, burning your eyes.

Panic rises in you.

Another flash of gold leaps out, visiting another blast of agony on your eyes. Regardless you follow the light further in. The corridor becomes so narrow, you are forced to move sideways. The gold light keeps flashing. After two hundred paces, you arrive at an intersection. One path flashes with the light. The other continues on into darkness. If you want to follow the golden light further, turn to **36**. If you prefer to continue along the dark corridor, turn to **31**.

24

You are only a few paces down into this dark passage when a sense of impending doom starts to weigh on you. A thought circulates, *What fool chooses the door marked with a cross? Surely death awaits*. You carry on, nonetheless. The Terrentine mystics have a saying about choices such as this: *Those who realise death, avoid the trap of hope*. Maybe the daunting path is the true path in this place. Maybe—

Your sword strikes something soft in the darkness.

Withdrawing the blade, you find it dry.

You reach a hand out.

Cloth. A heavy curtain draped across the passageway.

You tear it open and light spills in.

Turn to **39**.

25

The door marked with the spiral takes you into an unlit passage that soon grows too dark to safely navigate. You draw your sword and carry it aloft, tracking the wall with your spare hand. Moving this way is slow-going but after a period you sense that you are descending and that the wall is bowed. An unsettling sensation washes over: you are moving in a broad circle.

Hours later, you feel surer of this. The curvature of the

wall tightens and the slope of the floor feels steeper under-foot. You are spiralling down.

If the spiral door brought you here, you get to wondering about the alternate pathways foregone. Would the arrow passage have riddled you with arrows? Would the cross door lead you through to a burial cross or to a crossroads, to choices or options? On the spiral, your destination feels preordained.

You follow the path down and around until your body aches and throbs with fatigue. Time slips away inside the spiral and in the matte blackness there is no sense of movement or achievement. Wretched and desperate for rest, but fearful of this place, you push on and the passage keeps turning.

After many hours of staggering along, you finally trip and fall.

A sign.

You pad around the floor looking for sand or rat holes or any kind of opening that may allow the undead desert creatures in but find only a sealed corridor. Some part of you knows this is the way of this place.

This is a vacuum. A place of absence.

You rest your eyes.

You sleep.

You see dreams filled with ghosts set in an alien land. Everything in this setting is familiar but none of it makes linear sense. You feel things rather than know them. Are these memories, minced and reshaped? Have you lived so long without these thoughts that they now appear distant to you?

In the dream:

Two mirror women. Twins.

Erma.

Dora.

These names are known to you.

Their parents are there too, both as old as mystics and royalty.

A younger man also. A suitor.

He is called Euan.

Together they reside in a house made of impossible materials: surfaces and colours completely foreign. Walls with the white-ness of children's teeth. Window openings covered in transparent crystal, shaped like parchment. Steel shining like blade-iron but morphed into inconceivable shapes and forms: tiny instruments and fittings. And the sun shines with intense brightness in this place, making everything very clear. Everything in this world is flat and tamed. Even nature is forced to conform. This is a land of control.

Yet the connection between this diorama and your own world is not revealed in the dream. Instead, the objects and people are presented to you without story or context.

You wake parched and hungry and the world around you remains so unlit and barren of activity that you can't be sure your eyes are open. You take food and water from your dwindling supplies (you only have enough to sustain you for one more day) and you continue your descent, reaching for something in the dark. Increasingly, your thoughts wander. You think about the sisters from the dream. Dora and Erma. Strange names. Your mind returns to them constantly as you push on.

If you choose to dwell on Dora, turn to **37**. Or if you feel pulled towards the other one called Erma, turn to **34**.

26

You slowly lower a hand to the hilt of your sword and say, 'Not today.'

'Your loss, stranger,' says the creature, backing up. 'Perhaps I'll see you again soon?'

'I think not.'

You take careful steps past before breaking into a sprint. Minutes later, the corridor walls open up to accommodate a circular shaft. A conclusion. You lift a candle from a nearby lantern and drop it into the shaft. Brickwork all the way down until the candle hits water and ignites some type of fuel. A circle of flame fans out, illuminating the whole space. It looks to be a deep well of some sort with a rope hanging down the centre. And now, on the opposing side of this well, a good way down, you can see an opening in the wall.

Faced with the prospect of turning around and dealing with the lizard, you run and jump out. You fall a distance but your hands grab hold of the rope. The speed of your fall swings your body across, slamming your head and shoulder into the brickwork. Dazed and short of breath, you seize the rope between your legs and hold on, swaying back and forth until brick and mortar come loose above.

You drop.

As your legs plunge through the flaming waterline, you feel yourself transported.

Turn to **38**.

27

The curvature of the wall winds closer but the black endlessness of the passage continues. You start to fear for your mind. *How long can one go without light?* The only measure of time is the appearance of your monstrous hunger. This is a hunger born of at least three days without food. A dangerous hunger. Your sense of the world is slipping. There now exists a smooth gliding between vastly different states.

Asleep and awake.

Walking.

Sitting.

Lying.

Up.

Down.

None of it changes. None of it lights the path. You start to fear that this terrible descent is without end.

Until you notice a slight change in colour in the world around you. You can't be sure, but some of the darkness feels tempered.

Am I going blind?

You push on, drawing on a reserve of strength that you know is fraught.

The last gasp.

But the corridor lightens. It is not your mind playing tricks. You can see sand littering the floor now, the grit of the earthen walls.

You run until you collapse.

You sleep.

You get up and run again.

After episodes of unconsciousness and exertion blur into countless cycles, you finally step into the most unexpected of all chambers: the centre.

It is a small room, like the bottom of a well. And you can see clearly because the room forms a circle around a small candle-lit lantern. Beside the lantern is a basket of fresh fruit and a flask of wine. You grab the supplies and tears stream from your eyes as you take your first sip.

Once sated, you notice the strange symbols painted on the floor. A series of angular shapes. Small drawings of eyes, stars, machines, sea creatures. It's all marked in what looks like dried blood. You trace the designs with your hands and they all point to the lantern. Curious, you lift the lantern and underneath it is a tiny bowl of water. You dip a finger into this bowl and lift it to your mouth.

Sea water.

Something moves above you.

The round ceiling is descending.

Within seconds it is only a few feet from you. It looks like water. Black water. You jump into the air, puncturing the surface of this magical liquid, testing for a hard surface above. There is no such surface. It's all water.

The thought of stepping back into the spiral corridor is one you cannot bear, hence you stay in the room thinking, *If this is my end, unlord, then this is my end.* You conjure a fast death for yourself and watch the ceiling of water descend closer and closer. Eventually it reaches you and your outreached arms break the surface, like a diver in reverse. You swim up into it.

Turn to **38**.

28

The lizard-faced creature gives what you presume is a smile. 'You made yourself a good decision there, friend. A good decision. Now, step this way. You can call me Margo, if you like.' The look on your face must be clear because Margo smiles again and adds, 'Yeah, I was raised by damned fools. I know it. Who calls the likes of me Margo?'

Margo takes you down the little hallway and pushes aside another curtain, revealing a small cobblestone room. The room is furnished with a bench seat along one wall and a table against the other. There are two doors: one on the left that provides glimpses of Margo's quarters and another leading to descending stone steps. Steam drifts up out of the stair.

'OK now, do you need a robe or are you gonna wear that kit of yours in there?' Margo says, peering at you. 'Might be wise to wear your kit. It could use a steam. You can leave the rest up here.'

'No. It stays with me.'

Margo looks about to argue but says, 'It gets mighty hot down there.'

'Will I encounter anyone else?'

'One or two.'

'How many is that?'

'One or two. I don't work the morning shift. You know, it sounds like you need this sauna a mighty great deal. Now go on.'

You cross the room and pause at the mouth of the stair, feeling the heat rising up.

'Good luck,' says Margo.

'What do I need luck for?'

Margo doesn't answer.

You turn and look down into the heat and say, 'If there's danger here, danger of any kind, I'll come back up and kill you. You know this, yes?'

'All travellers need a bit of luck, for crying out loud. I say it to damn near everyone. Now will you get a move on before I refund your money with that crossbow of mine.'

You take the first step.

Turn to **40**.

29

The ogre moves like a grounded bat, a heaving mass of muscle but uneven in its gait. The thing dips its head and screams with ungodly force.

To begin, the smaller of the two creatures sprints out to the side – fangs glistening – and leaps into the air. You parry left and bring the sword across in a wide sweep. The tip of your weapon catches the beast and drops it like a stone. It emits a terrible whimper. With your eyes fixed on the mother, you step across and strike the smaller creature again, skewering it to be sure. As you withdraw the sword, it's heavy with entrails.

No mercy.

Not for the likes of this.

The mother screeches again. It seems less sure of itself now. It moves forward and back in the water.

'Come now, beast. It's your time.'

You charge the ogre and leap into the air, throwing your sword into the creature's face. The blade hits square and topples it. You land on its torso and grab the sword as the creature's flailing arms thrash at you. You rip the sword around in a wide arc, removing arms and claws before getting down to the grisly work of finishing the ogre off. A certain blankness takes over.

Muscle memory.

Physical work. Like digging post holes or a grave.

Some tinge of history repeating . . .

When you're done, the room falls quiet. The water runs thick and oily with blood. You splash around searching for guarded treasure or secret hatches. There is none of this – the walls are bare – but there is a nest of sorts: a submerged mound of clay and shit, decorated with the bones of unlucky travellers. You reach into the nest and clench your hand around what feels like a large rock. As you tug on the rock, a beam of green light blasts out of the mound. In horror, you watch as your arm evaporates into dust. The room tilts. The smell of singed flesh fills your nostrils. Your face lands in the water and the world goes dark.

Humans sit around a table, eating. A family. A father, a mother and two younger women, two daughters who look the same. Twins. But there is another, a young man. The way he's sitting and touching one of the twins – a hand gently resting on the back of her neck – he's no brother. A suitor. He looks around the table and says something but you cannot hear this scene.

The father responds, smiling.

The mother laughs.

One girl nods.

But the other sister, she glares across the table, moving from one person to the next. The suitor looks directly at her and speaks. The girl moves without warning. She steps up from the table, her left hand wrapped around a dinner fork. She swings out.

The father springs up.
The mother screams and screams.

You come up fast and vomit water and ogre blood all over yourself before moving into a coughing jag unlike any other. Every inch of your frame wracks in violent seizure. A part of your mind knows that death has visited you briefly. You almost drowned.

You must be in a state of shock because it's minutes before you realise that your arm is still intact. It has rematerialised. Terrified, you scurry away from the nest, past the bodies of the slain ogres and back to the stairs. It is only after you have climbed the stairs, arriving again in the large grey cavernous room, that you start to calm yourself. The white crystal poles at the far end of the room start to glow, calling you.

Turn to **42**.

30

It is a short stair and from the top you can hear running water. Despite being this far underground, some sort of natural light shines up.

'Hello?'

Your voice echoes.

No response.

At the bottom of the stairs, you survey a broad space about the size of a church hall but with a low, flat ceiling. A thousand lanterns flicker just above head height, all strung to the roof. At your feet, the floor is covered in fast-moving water, bright with the lustre of the lanterns. Off to one side, you notice an object. A shrouded presence.

'Show yourself,' you say, gripping your sword.

The presence unwraps itself.

No.

This cannot be.

The creature spreads its wretched talons to full width. It looks to be some kind of deformed ogre: a humanoid but with four arms and a light fur-like covering. The thing roars and another creature, smaller yet of precisely the same design, steps out from behind the first. Milk drips from its mouth. Some horrible family of violence and mayhem.

If you choose to stay and fight, turn to **29**.

If you choose to flee, turn to **41**.

31

The passage arcs around to your right. It remains narrow and dark and grows only darker as the golden light recedes in the distance. After a time, the roof lowers gradually, forcing you to hunch down and crawl. The ground beneath your hands and knees starts as dirt but transitions into some kind of stone paving dotted with hundreds of holes the size of pebbles. As you crawl further into the passage, warm steam rises up from the holes in the floor. The steam is gentle, a comfortable wash of heat and moisture. You feel as if you could lie in the passage a while.

I could take my rest here.

Your eyes are heavy.

Just a moment . . .

Without much thought, you lower yourself to the ground and dream.

Two women, the same age and with the same features. The same hair, the same brow, the same eyes. One is wounded: bruised with bandaged limbs. The other is unharmed. They appear to be sitting in a garden the likes of which is foreign to you. Ornate flowers grow in the heat.

One of the girls has tears in her eyes. She says, 'What do you mean, Euan isn't who he says he is?' It's the one with the bandaged limbs.

'He's not right for you, Dora. There's another side to him.'

'What did he do?'

'It's not one thing. Have you noticed how he looks at me? I don't like being around him.'

'Erma, that's not—'

'I don't know how you can stand to have him around.'

'Why? Because he's more interested in me than you? Is that it? Oh poor fucking Erma.'

They sit beside each other silently for a minute.

The one called Erma speaks first. 'Mum said that you two were—'

'It's true. He asked. I'm thinking about it.'

213

'That's completely insane. What does Mum think?'

'Why would she have a problem with it?'

'So you're actually considering it? Dora, it's not the time to get married. Even if he were the one.'

'Not the time? Look at me! If he wants me like this, isn't that a measure of something? And besides, I want to get married. I'm not like you. I don't want to just have, I don't know, choices. I don't want that. Not after all this.'

'Dad says he's after our money.'

'Dad says that about everyone.'

'It's a mistake.'

'What would you know?' Dora sister wipes at her eyes. 'I'm serious. Tell me, what would you know?'

'Nothing. Forget it.'

'That's right,' says Dora. 'That's your answer to everything.'

Your body jolts awake before your mind. You feel a cool breeze on your arms and orbs of light float above you, out past your closed eyelids. You look and it's all gone: the twin sisters, the garden, the argument, the light. You're surprised to find yourself standing in a coal-black void. You reach out and touch the world, finding a wall of cloth. A curtain. You open it and light seeps in.

Turn to **39**.

32

You come to coughing and roll onto your side to heave air. You find yourself in a new room. The sand, the ghost and the bronze panel have all disappeared. The new space is still triangular in shape but the walls are made of dark maroon clay. The ceiling above does not pulse with light but instead appears coated in sand. You know, without understanding how, that you are in the chamber below.

You stand.

You study the walls.

There's an opening cut into one corner of the room and past that a corridor of strange dimensions. The corridor is impossibly tall – as tall as the sky – but runs only a short distance before sharply hooking right into another hallway and another sharp right and then the same again, and again.

You run these halls.

Right and then right and then right, each turn bringing you to a longer passage. A triangular-shaped maze, spiralling out. As you move along the corridors, you begin to hear something, a low humming sound. It grows in intensity with each turn. The floor begins to vibrate. You enter a final long straight passageway and run towards the sound. As you move, the walls begin to close around you, collapsing inward. A threshold approaches. It is grey beyond, the colour of slate.

You sprint.

The walls brush your shoulders, squeezing in.

The grey threshold grows larger and the sound amplifies until it's an earth-rending roar, a blasting cacophony.

You dive.

Then nothing.

Silence.

The grey room.

The corridor seals silently shut behind you.

This new chamber is the opposite of that which came before. It's a wide chasm. Three of the walls are square but the one opposite is curved, as if this whole hall is wrapped around a giant cylinder.

On your left, down the far end of the grey hall, two white crystal poles stand a short distance apart. Both are carefully machined and each are the height of a tall human. The poles look completely alien in this muted space. Up the other end of the chamber, you find a rectangular hole in the floor and a set of stairs leading down out of view. If you'd like to investigate the crystal poles, turn to **42**. If you'd prefer to take the stairs down to the next level, turn to **30**.

1203

I've been in here for four days now. Or five. Or six. Less than a week. While I struggle to stay calm and think my way out of this, I'm haunted by bad episodes from my life.

Haunted by Dora.

I can't fight it.

All the choices are gone now. What's left are scenes without structure. My life disassembled. Fantasies so warped and real in this place without reality that I can't tell Sero's world from my own. I'm not sure I want to. I'm not sure the line is clear anymore. How can reality be clear when the fantasy barbarian dreams of me instead of the other way around?

I'm unravelling.

I'm seeing things I pushed from view.

I see this, for example:

Down dark corridors of my old house, through the room beside the upstairs study and the bathroom my father always used. It's the middle of the night. I can't sleep because the pain in my legs is so bad I can't lie still.

There's a small window in this bathroom by the study. I crack it and light a joint, hoping it'll get me through to my next dose of Percocet. This window – in the small room – is really a window into a whole new world, because from this small window, in the bathroom my father always used, I can see into the cottage at the back of the property. I can see my mother fucking Euan on the floor of the cottage. I can see her hair and her arse and Euan's legs.

I close the window.

I sit on the closed pedestal.

Work on the joint.

Ignore the window.

But then I stand and reopen it and look again, to be sure, and I see something different. It's not my mother. It's my sister. The meds are fucking with me.

I stare out.

Dora's hair.

Dora's arse.

And the legs of . . .
Ryan Solis.
No, David Brier.
No, Dylan Copson.
No, Euan.
What?
What's happening?
I close the portal and look into the mirror and Dora's there behind me like a ghost from a horror film, her eyes staring into my eyes, her lips cold and cruel.

'Hi.'

'Jesus fucking Christ, Dora.'

'What are you doing in here?' *my sister says, and without warning she slams her fist into the side of my skull.*

33

A pulse of light fires down and smoke from the vaporised vial rockets into your lungs. You take a heroic toke and hold the smoke. The burn is incredible.

What is this vile poison?

The ghost holds out his hand for the mouthpiece.

He takes it and drags on the remainder. You watch as smoke fills his transparent throat and hovers in the space where his lungs should be. He gasps. 'It's good shit.'

You both exhale together.

'Shall we dance?' says the ghost and, without warning, he walks into you then turns, covering your arms and legs with his sorcery. As you wave a hand covered in his hand, his voice says, *Let me show you how to be a ghost, let me show you how to haunt . . .*

In the white sky, a burning star. Summer. And under it, a monument of some kind – a house perhaps – and a green garden and a pool. By the pool, a girl in scant garments and dark eyeglasses. She has a book. The girl puts the book down and rolls a set of dice across a small glass-topped table.

Eight.

And a four.

Twelve.

She shrugs and notes the number down in her book with a pencil.

She rolls again.

A one and a two.

'Erma!' comes a voice across the yard. 'Erma, where are you?'

'Down here.'

An older woman and a man make their way down the stairs and into the paved area around the pool. They stop at the younger woman's feet. Two figures, casting a shadow.

'Who's this?' says the girl.

'This is Euan. He's going to be moving into the cottage and looking after odds and ends around here. He's David Reyner's son.'

'Nice to meet you David Reyner's son,' says the girl. She raises her book. 'The pool needs a clean. The guy didn't come yesterday.'

'Sorry,' says the woman. 'Politeness isn't my daughter's strong suit.'

'I can clean it,' says Euan.

In the pool beside them, the water ripples lightly; it's a light blue, cast by a narrow rim of similarly coloured tiles just above the waterline. Down beneath the surface, there is a bright steel drain set flush into the pearl-white floor. It glistens in the sun.

You feel your chest tighten. You feel like you're choking. Turn to **32**.

34

Erma paces in an alleyway lined with iron containers spilling paper and glass. A demonic thump comes from one wall of this alley. It's raining but Erma seems immune to the weather. She paces, clenches her fist. A portal in the wall opens and the sound that spills out fills you with dread. Surely this is a place of malicious spirits and wizardry.

A woman arrives via the portal and it slams closed behind her. 'What?' she screams. 'What do you want?'

Erma says, 'I want what I paid you for. Why are you doing this to me?'

The woman is young. She laughs, then leans into the wall for cover and lights a cigarette. 'I could ask you the same question.'

Erma steps in close and the resemblance is made clear. They both have similar hair, similar eyes, similar bones. They could be sisters.

'Jenny, all I ever did was help you.'

'If that's what you call help, I'd hate to see what harm is. And now, you're going to cough up that extra cash or you can do your own fucking—'

Erma's punch is fast and effective. Jenny folds over: she's bent double and she retches until she heaves a pint of ale onto the floor of the alleyway. Erma grabs her around the throat and slams her head back into the wall.

'Hand over that fucking data, Jenny.'

The girl laughs and cries at the same time. 'Or what? You'll beat me up?'

'Yes.' Erma squeezes her throat. 'You could have been just like me, Jenny. I would have done everything in this world to help you but you had to go and mess it up.'

Jenny starts to claw at the hand around her throat.

Erma lets her go.

'I'm getting on a plane to Spain tomorrow. You better have that stuff for me by the time I get back or there will be hell to pay. And clean yourself up. You look like garbage.'

Turn to **27**.

35

A pulse of light fires down and smoke rockets up the hose. You take a short toke and cough the rest of it out. The ghost shakes his head. His disapproval is the last thing you see before you find yourself melting into the floor, falling down into some hellish new dimension.

★

The hole they have Erma in is as unlit as the dungeon corridors. It smells of bleach and mould; of damp, dank furniture and fabric. Like a rotten motel. There are no coordinates for this place, no bearings. It's been pure darkness since the moment the hood covered her face.

You float like a ghost watching over her.

Two days of this nothingness. It breaks her down.

The door opens, and, beyond, there's a drab hallway, the hum of harsh fluorescent bulbs, the sense of a place underground; then in the doorway, a tall, thin woman in a black dress.

'If you want to get out of here, you need to learn to kneel when you hear me coming,' she says as she slops food down on the floor.

The room is tiled in white.

There's a drain in the centre.

You feel your chest throttled by pain.

Turn to **32**.

36

The path leads you downwards and the golden light keeps coming, faster and faster, brighter and brighter. During one blinding flash, you lose your footing and fall, shredding your arms and hands as you roll and skid. You tumble down the corridor and free-fall into a vast chamber filled with thick flaxen mist. The mist is heavy and it slows your descent, lowering you to the bottom of what appears to be a tall triangular pit.

Three giant walls rise up around you. They converge to form a small triangular apex. That apex throbs and glows before blasting down a wave of light so harsh it forces your eyes closed. As the room comes back into view, you find that you are no longer alone. A cloaked figure stands in the mist.

'Who goes there?'

The mist parts. The figure is an old man, feet bare in the sand. He appears completely unafraid. He comes closer and you notice an unusual shimmer to him and recoil. He is transparent. You stab at him with your sword and it passes through him as if dipped in water.

'Having fun?' he says.

'A ghost. This place is without reason.'

'Yes, yes. I have some bad news for you if you're afraid of ghosts. There are a lot of us down here. The whole set-up is run by ghosts. Ghosts and demons. All very . . . er, hold on. Close your eyes.'

You refuse. The triangle above bathes the room again, blinding you a second time. When the blindness recedes, the ghost remains.

'Life is wasted on the stupid,' he says. 'Now, I believe you have something for me. You wouldn't be called down here otherwise.'

'I have nothing for the likes of you, unlord.'

The ghost sighs and holds open his hand. A small triangular tube appears in the air above his palm. It rotates slowly in the air. The tube is identical to the yellow vial you've carried with you this whole journey, since the orcs slain in the forest.

'Hand it over,' he says.

'What is it? Tell me.'

'Troll piss. And aged cider. You can have it back, don't worry.'

You retrieve the vial and hold it out for the ghost to see.

'Yes,' the ghost says, studying the vial. 'That'll fit.'

'I was told not to drink it.'

'And you didn't drink it, that's a surprise.'

The ghost sweeps his robes up and walks towards the centre of the chamber. He kneels down beside a bronze panel in the floor and sweeps sand from the surface, configuring a set of dials and switches on the panel. A small hatch opens: a triangular slot precisely the shape and size of the vial.

'Go on, slip it in.'

You approach the panel and do as requested. The vial goes all the way down without friction. The bronze panel hums. The ghost scratches around in the sand for what at first glance looks like a buried rope. On closer inspection it is a bronze chain-mail hose. At the end of the hose is a moulded mouthpiece resembling the head of a snake.

The ghost says, 'Now, when the light up there comes on again, this contraption will cook up that vial and push it down this tube. You can either breathe in a little or a lot, the choice is yours.' The ghost cocks his head, squints up at the ceiling. 'OK, here we go.'

If you choose to inhale a little, turn to **35**.

If you choose to inhale a lot, turn to **33**.

37

Dora is the twin with the suitor and you feel an immediate connection with her. Her sense of the world aligns with your own. There is a dark ease with which she deals with obstruction – you sense this – and like yourself, she is trapped. Or feels trapped. At present, her body is damaged from a war you cannot comprehend. Her memories reveal a terrible event: the day Dora rode in the belly of an iron carriage, hurtling through the world with a speed beyond that of the fastest horse, fuelled by some occult power, until a collision of horrifying force: metal bending around her, pinning her limbs, puncturing and tearing at her to the point where she is now bedridden.

Trapped.

Incapacitated.

In her own spiral.

Dora slips in and out of hazy visions and terrifying nightmares of pressure and burn. Day and night blend together. Liquid food. Hot sweats and creatures growling, gnawing at her. And somewhere in there, a faceless figure standing over her bed, naked from the waist down.

Turn to **27**.

38

You wake and find yourself laid out on a marble floor slick with trickling saltwater. Overhead, a thousand decorative lanterns hang down, giving the room a strangely warm sheen despite the cold.

Am I dead?

You find your strength and get to your feet. The room around you is empty and square. A thin film of water seeps through a portal in one wall, across the floor and out a similar sized drain on the other side. The flickering lanterns above seem to serve no purpose.

There is a door. A set of steps leading up. You climb halfway up the steps and carefully survey the cavernous chamber above. It's a long space. One wall is straight but the opposing one bows out as if bulging under some godlike force. A pair of strange illuminated poles stand at the far end of this room, past the apex of the bulging wall. The poles are shaped from a white crystalline substance.

It appears safe. The room below you gives you the fear. There is something off about a room that has water flowing across the floor and lanterns above. It's mismatched. No good could come of it.

You go to the hall.

Turn to **42**.

39

Lanterns dot the corridor ahead. Timber slats are laid into the flooring. You set out and your footsteps fall into a bracing rhythm, the air around you buzzing with dust and lantern fuel. After a time, you spot a change in the passage ahead. A brighter lantern fixed to the wall. An opening beside it.

'Who goes there?' you shout, announcing yourself.

A torso leans out into the corridor and calls back, 'Stranger, I'll have none of that kind of trouble in here. This is a place of relaxation for tired travellers. Put that sword away or turn back.'

'I'll do no such—'

An arrow thuds into the wall by your shoulder. The force of it suggests a crossbow.

'A place of relaxation, I said. Now be calm.'

You re-sheathe your sword and walk closer with hands raised.

'That's better,' says the voice. 'What are you? Man or woman?'

'What are you?' is your response.

It steps out of its hole. The creature stands upright on two stumpy human legs but has the tail and face of a reptile. Its eyes are pure evil (thin black pupils surrounded by a pus-coloured yellow iris) and yet the mouth is the worst of it: a garish mess of broken fangs and dripping saliva. A pink forked tongue slides in and out without warning.

'Pretty, ain't I?' says the creature. It holds a crossbow lazily in one hand.

'What is this place?'

'This? Why this, my friend, is the best sauna this side of Ulteron. Got the finest hot room in the whole province, if you ask me. You need a rest, stranger? This is the place. If you've got the gold, that is?'

'I'm here for the . . .' and you struggle to picture the water from Rohank's vision. 'The lake. Is there an underground lake somewhere in this dungeon?'

'This ain't no dungeon,' says the creature. 'But sure, we've got ourselves a lake. I draw my sauna from it every day. How else you figure I run a business down here? Now, you gonna show me that gold or not? Because I ain't got time to stand out here all day firing arrows and gasbaggin'.'

If you choose to take a sauna, turn to **28**.

If you wish to keep on your way, turn to **26**.

40

The sauna is a seamless stone box about the size of a horse's stable. It's situated in the centre of a much larger room, every surface of which is slick with moisture. Banks of mist surround the sauna, giving it a gloomy feel. The interior is bracingly hot and as your eyes adjust you notice the place is lit by red molten rocks arranged in a pit on the floor. Sitting on the other side of this rock pile are three figures. There is an old man with a pale beard and a sprawl of dark tattoos running the length of his chest. Beside him is a younger woman built like a pit fighter. Then a full-grown orc sitting apart from the couple.

The woman says, 'You best put that sword down, if you wish to stay in here. That is, if you call that a sword.'

'She's right,' says the old man, 'there's no need for that thing. Besides, Seelap down there has a touch of the mage about him and he isn't too friendly this time of day, not when it comes to stolen swords.'

The orc grunts.

'I'm none too friendly either,' you say.

'Then get the fuck out of here,' says the woman. 'We were here first.'

'Or you could sit down and be quiet,' says the man. 'You look as though some time in here would do you good. We're easy company in the right circumstances.'

You remain standing.

The orc holds a hand aloft. A bright blue orb materialises around his closed fist. He grunts again.

'That's your last warning,' says the woman. She stretches her neck side to side.

'Please sit,' says the man.

There's no deciding which one of these three poses the biggest threat. The orc is obviously capable of all manner of mayhem but the mage class orcs tend to be less violent. They're healers. And magic in a confined space such as this would put the whole party in peril. The woman, on the other hand, looks formidable in exactly this sort of place. She could be on you in seconds. And then there's the old man. He's the type to have a concealed weapon. An ex-soldier or mercenary. The sort that never relies on luck or goodwill.

You take a seat across from them.

'Where are you from?' says the man.

'Where are you going?' adds the woman before you can answer.

'I'm looking for a dark lake.'

'He has a spiral on him,' says the orc. 'On his back. I can see through this one.'

It feels odd to hear the orc speak your language.

'Where are you from, friend?' repeats the man.

'I'm without memory. I could be from anywhere.'

'Maybe you're from here?' says the orc.

'Maybe you should cease using your demon magic on me or you'll find your own self in need of healing.'

'I look but I don't touch,' says the orc.

'Ain't the first time I've heard that down here,' says the woman.

The man makes a wry smile. 'You know, one without memory or destination can oft find themselves in a place like this. You should be careful. Might be that such a place is seeking you more than the other way around.'

'You speak in tongues, old man.'

'Tell me about it,' says the woman. 'Now, if you could all shut the hell up, I want Seelap to get this pit fired up.'

On cue, the orc stands and draws a ladle of water from a chute built into the wall. 'This is from the lake,' he says with a smile and, as he pours the water over the coals, the room turns a thick primary red like fresh blood. The heat comes at you, a wave of infernal damnation, a message from the black world. Your skin slides loose from your body.

'What have you done?' you snarl.

No answer arrives.

You feel yourself falling, disappearing down through the stone bench as if it were an apparition. You scramble for your sword, catching it just as you tumble down through the floor of the sauna, through the stone and dirt, into the void below. As your body passes through the world, you fall into the thoughts of a stranger.

A woman and her mother sit in a room filled with trinkets and oddly shaped tools. The room is completely foreign, some kind of indoor heaven filled with white surfaces and morning light.

'You're what?' says the mother.

'Pregnant,' says the woman.

'How? You're not. You don't even have a boyfriend.'

The girl has drinking pottery in her hand. She stares down into it and says, 'That's not important right this fucking second.'

'Don't use that language with me,' says the mother.

'I think we're a bit past that.'

'Oh, you do, do you?'

'I want to get rid of it.'

'Jesus,' says the mother. 'How did this happen?'

'Fuck, Mum, the usual way, OK? Are you going to help me or not?'

The mother breathes slow. 'What are you asking me, Erma? What are you asking me?'

In another dimension, you feel cold, as if immersed in mountain water. Turn to **38**.

41

Fuelled only by instinct, you let out a quiet shushing sound, as if tending to an infant. As you make the sound, you slowly back away. The creatures screech again, in unison. You take another step. And another. The bigger one rolls its shoulders but neither of them moves to attack. You retreat up the stairs and at the top you are so fixated on the danger avoided that you walk backwards another thirty paces before crumpling to the ground and vomiting onto the grey slate floor. Once rested, you turn your attention to the only other thing in the room: the white crystal poles. Turn to **42**.

42

As you make your way up the room, the poles start to change colour, from white to a rich throbbing red. You circle them carefully, quite sure that they will shoot fire or lightning or trigger some other calamitous event. You hold a hand out to them without result. They do not emit heat or magic. You look above them to the towering ceiling and find only darkness. Your eyes cannot see that far, not to the top. Perplexed, you head back down the room, stepping between the poles for the first time.

The poles flicker out like blown candles.

The room begins to move under your feet. The walls rumble and dust falls from the seams. You watch as a monolithic wall panel, tall and wide as a dam, slides open. The force of the movement is so immense, so hard to comprehend, that you feel raw adrenaline take hold.

This is the work of inhuman forces.

It cannot be.

What black magic governs this place?

Light erupts from the opening. Birdsong echoes. Then, from the hole, comes a mist of something familiar. It sweeps out on a strong wind and wets your face. It's rain. *How is it raining in a dungeon?* You walk into the gale and see towering brown columns rise up. Over the threshold of the giant doorway, the ground becomes soft underfoot. This is foliage. The giant portal leads into some kind of forest that is thick and tall and real. Rain continues to drift down from a white ceiling high above, full of glare and brightness. You cannot see the dungeon walls containing this garden. These are immense trees for indoors. Impossible trees.

You continue into the forest and follow a small ridge-line that gently sweeps up from the floor. Within minutes, you cannot see the giant door behind you; the jungle is far too dense for that. You wander down through undulating country. As the rain comes gradually heavier, you find yourself drawn down an incline into a small clearing. In the clearing, you find a cave. A dark hole in the hillside.

A sickening emptiness blossoms in your gut.

You know this place.

You have been to this forest before.

You remember this cave.

'No,' you say. 'No.'

This is the same forest. The same cave. This is the land you started out from. That is the cave from which you woke, all laid out in this dungeon like an occult replica or . . .

No!

This cannot pass.

It cannot be.

You have never left this place.

ERMA

They keep me in a room the length of a coffin. Tiles on the floor. A drain in the centre. No light. Once a day – give or take – the door opens and a thin woman in a black dress gives me water and rice. I eat with my hands. I cry for help. I thrash at the walls and beg. The rest of the time, I lie in the darkness and dream of the barbarian. Sero remains locked inside me.

They pull me out. There's two of them. Two men. I recognise one. He's the guy from the car shed. *Drew*. I've had the time to put Drew's name to his face, to remember him. Drew is the guy from the pub way back at the start, the one who tried to pick up Jenny's sister. Mister Glasses-Or-No-Glasses. *They make everyone look smarter.* And here's the kicker, he's also An*drew* from my favourite Missing Person flyer, as well. The flyer in my handbag, wherever that is. Drew and I have been circling each other all this time.

Drew and the other man – both wearing surgical masks against the smell of my piss and shit-stained clothes – drag me out of the box while I scream for help. Drew's eyes tighten as he grabs at me, yelling for me to shut the hell up. He works quickly to pull me out and along a corridor by my ankles. I scream again. I sense movement and scan around. My eyes are fucked but through the haze I can see three girls standing at the end of the corridor as I'm dragged towards them. The girls are all wearing white surgical gowns. No shoes. Three of them, the same: bright red hair, shoulder length. All three of them wearing identical black spectacles.

I scream for help but they step aside as I'm dragged past. I see flashes of the room:

Bunk beds.

A grubby kitchenette. A circular table.

Walls thick with dirt.

Soundproofing and cheap carpet.

A bunker.

I feel the sting of a needle behind my right knee. It's the other man. The man who helped Drew haul me out of my cell. And now I recognise him from before, from however long ago, from the house, the car shed. *The doctor.* I grab for his arm as he withdraws the syringe and I pull him down into my closed fist. I'm weak but he keels over, clutching his throat. Drew drops one of my legs in the struggle and it's all I need. I twist the foot he's holding and pull it out of his grip, turning my body and getting ready to stand. I get halfway into a crouch when my legs soften. I shout something to the girls but it comes out garbled and underwater. They're clearer now:

The same nose and cheekbones.
The same lips.
Beautiful, in another setting.
They're all very thin, very gaunt.
Three daughters.
That's the last thing.

The rest is chaotic and dreamlike. I'm sitting down but moving. The skin on my face hot and thick. There's greenery and sunlight, then shade, then a booming voice and a hand patting my hand and knee before the sting of another needle and then more movement, breeze on my skin, the tinny tone of a dictaphone playing back and electronic sounds and a keypad and a door closing and I'm back in my coffin, back in the darkness where I'm thrashed around by nightmares and memory.

Days pass in the hole but I'm not like I was at the start. I'm relaxed and compliant now. I stop screaming. I spend my life asleep, dreaming of Sero and the fantasy world. I start to feel this is where I belong.

And I can't really remember anything else.

I think they've taken me out a few more times now.

I hear whispers.

I have visions.

Or, I should say, I feel them because they're without detail. All contour. No reason or story.

Endless.

I see the door open.

Drew and the doctor are standing there.

The doctor has a taser in his hand.

He reaches out.

Sparks fire.

I stop drinking the water. I don't know why. Some reason. Something deep down inside, a soft voice that tells me it's poison. I don't drink poison. I remember that much, at least.

★

I see the door open and sound floods in: voices and music and footsteps. A group of men, a party, coming from upstairs. The thin woman in the black dress steps into the door frame. She has something in her hand, a beam of light.

Another silhouette pops into view, just a head.

'See,' says the woman. 'I told you she was bleeding. You picked a bad time of the month for this little shindig.'

The lights go out.

I see the door open.

A man and a hose.

The water is like a waterfall blasting down from some mountain creek but, as good as it is, I'm sobbing through it, terrified but not so terrified that I don't take secret sips.

I see the door open and they drag me out and I don't know why. I don't know how long I'm away but I know I've been outside when I return. There's dirt in my eyes. And aches and scabs.

I come to and my head is bobbing violently, straining the muscles of my neck.

I'm outside.

Grey sky.

Shrubs.

Flowers.

Clean air.

The crunch of gravel.

I try to move my arms but they're fastened to armrests. I realise I'm strapped to a wheelchair.

'Where, where is this?'

'Doctor Bridges, are you awake? Oh my.'

Harlan's voice. Archibald's assistant. I can't see him. He might be the one pushing me.

'Yeah, I'm awake.'

'That's interesting,' he says.

My vision firms up. I watch the garden peel away as we come along the crest of a tapering grass hill. A chilly wind comes up off the hill, nipping at my skin, my eyes, my ears, my mouth. *Something's wrong. Something's covering my face.* I use my peripherals and see brown blurs around the rims of my eye sockets. They have me in some kind of mask.

'Here we are,' says Harlan.

We enter a small grove of kurrajong trees, a green canopy swaying.

'Not much of a day for it,' says Harlan.

I tug at my restraints. My legs are trapped too.

In the clearing under the trees, Archibald Moder sits in a camp chair. He has a walking cane between his legs, a Thermos by his feet, two steel mugs set up on a flattened timber stump beside the chair. 'Ah, Erma. How are you today? Good I hope,' he says as I'm parked in front of him. He reaches over and pats my hand. 'They're predicting rain so we might have to be quick today.'

'What have you done to my face?'

Before he can answer, Harlan says, 'She seems more alert than usual. I'll talk to Sadie about it.'

'That's fine, that's fine,' says Archibald. 'I'll be OK. Actually, no. Do you have that contraption with you, Harlan?'

'What contraption?' he says.

'The little camera. Come take a photo of her.'

Harlan leans over Archibald's shoulder and aims a digital camera at me. The lens buzzes. He checks the screen and takes another photo.

'Now show her,' says Archibald. 'Dear child, this is what happens when you try to bite Doctor Dalloway.'

I don't remember biting anyone but my jaw has ached for a few days now. I look at the camera screen and my heart begins to race. I'm wearing a brown leather mask, a crude, home-made thing. At the mouth, there is a grey mesh grill weaved in. The mask is strapped to my head with a series of belts and buckles.

'What is this? Where am I?'

'I can take it from here,' says Archibald.

Harlan's footsteps fade.

Archibald says, 'You must be thirsty.' He pours black tea into a cup with a straw. With some difficulty, he unstraps one of my wrists so I can drink. Once I have the tea in hand, I swallow it in one long pull.

'You *are* thirsty, then?'

'Fuck you.'

'Erma.'

'If I ever get this other hand—'

'Stop! Erma!' Archibald withdraws a notebook from his pocket. 'I need you to comport yourself today. I'm expecting a guest. I'm afraid I'm going to have to reprimand you for that. It's tiresome but you've scarcely given me a choice.'

Archibald slowly gets to his feet. His eyes harden.

'Archie?' I say.

He stands beside me and I watch with slow dread as he loosens the belt of his grey crimplene pants. He slides the belt free and the pants fall. And then Archibald Moder, the man I spent years studying, folds his belt in two and brings it down across my bare thighs.

Thwack.

I scream.

Thwack.

Thwack.

Thwack.

I keep screaming. I'm scratching at my constraints with my free hand. I need to move, to get away, but it's pointless – *thwack, thwack, thwack* – each blow coming faster and faster. Spit flies from Archibald's mouth and eventually I close down. I stop struggling. I don't know how long it lasts but, by the end of it, I'm immobile, my eyes squeezed shut, letting it happen.

'Now, where were we?' he says, wheezing.

I reopen my eyes.

Moder is back in his chair, wiping my blood from his

hands with a handkerchief. His pants remain around his ankles. 'Oh yes. The drinking. Why aren't you drinking your water, Erma? You'll die if you refuse water. You know that, don't you?'

'I was . . . I don't want to die.'

'No one wants you to die, Erma. We've made fine progress here. Fine progress. Up until recently you were doing well. We were working on that temper, that violence in you. And it was going very, very well, I'd say. Do you know you were doing so well?'

'I can't remember anything.'

'That's the medication.'

'What do you want with me? Why are you doing this?'

'What do you mean?'

'Let me go. I don't want to be here.'

'Oh Erma. I can't do that. I let your friend go before she was ready and look how that turned out. No, no. We need to push on. Your sessions have really been progressing well. Last week, you were finally starting to open up. Can you remember our chat about your family?'

I shake my head. I'm slipping away, going into some kind of shock, letting something delayed take hold. Blood trickles down my legs, drips onto my feet.

Archibald gets his notebook back out and says, 'You told me about Euan, your twin sister's boyfriend. The man who got you pregnant.'

'Not . . . we aren't twins.'

'Go on.'

'We're not, I mean, no. *No*. Fuck you! *Fuck you!* I'm going to fucking kill you, Archie. I'm going to—' and I still have a hand free so I lash out. I reach out and try to claw at him but am nowhere near close enough to land a blow. Archibald swats me away with his belt. He catches me around the neck and shoulders with more stinging blows but it doesn't stop me. I struggle until I manage to drag my chair over, slamming myself into the dirt.

In the distance, I hear Harlan hollering.

'You're right. She's not herself today,' Moder says.

My body is hoisted back up with the chair. It isn't gentle. Harlan clamps my free hand and straps it back in. He puts another belt around my chest. I'm completely pinned. 'Are we going to punish her?' he says to Archibald. 'I want to.'

'I don't know. Erma? Erma!' Archibald moves forward on his camp chair. 'Can you behave yourself, please. Can you?'

Getting no reply, he nods to Harlan.

Electricity crackles.

A bolt of agony blasts through my side, snapping my body into a rigid contortion.

I can't breathe.

I can't breathe.

This is it. A seizure. A heart attack.

Something.

But then the pain relents as fast as it arrived. I slump back in the wheelchair and take deep breaths. I want to vomit but I'm too scared.

'Keep that thing out. Just in case.' says Archibald. 'Now take that wretched mask off.'

Harlan dumps something in my lap and works on the mask. When the mask comes free, I look down and see I'm nursing a taser. Harlan picks it up and waves it in front of my face. 'Bitch, you try to hit Dad again, I will fry you like a roast chook.'

'Harlan, please,' says Archibald.

Harlan walks away. I want to follow his movements, scared he'll tase me from behind a second time, but my restraints are too tight and I can't swivel far enough around to see him. My mind races. Archibald's talking to me, asking questions that I can't really hear. My ears are trained on Harlan. This is all animal instinct now. Survival mode.

I hear a sound coming from Harlan's direction. Wheels in gravel. Footsteps in gravel. Another wheelchair coming and all the while Archibald prattles on, ' . . . and I really think it best if you open up further about this because, as you know from my work, human behaviour is a set of choices. That's all it is. But, Erma, we don't always make them, that's the thing. Sometimes there are other aspects of our lives that dictate the choices, things that *set* the choices, Erma. Erma, are you listening to me?'

The second wheelchair can't be more than a few feet away.

'Erma?'

'Yes?' I say.

'Are you listening?'

'Yes.'

'Your life is like one of my books. Everyone's is. There is no infinite amount of choice, as we all imagine. We think there is but, in fact, our choices are extremely narrow, almost to the point of no choice at all. Do you know that a gamebook is composed of about four hundred sections? That's it. Just four hundred sections. That's the entire universe of a gamebook. And yet it feels free compared to a regular novel, doesn't it? Such a liberation. But it's not, is it?'

I shake my head. The other wheelchair draws closer.

'Four hundred moments to choose from. That's fate. That's what it is. Fate's the thing we never want to talk about. We have all the free will in the world and nowhere to put it, because of fate. I mean, look at us. Look at us, Erma. In our case, there's a through line, a red thread, a fishing line bringing you to me, isn't there? If you look back, it's always been there. Always. You read my books as a child and now here you are. You chose this, in a round-about way. Just as there is an intersecting line steering me to you, to here, to this very spot, something *I* chose from my limited options.' Archibald waves to someone behind me. 'What I'm saying is, fate is real, Erma. The red thread. It brought us here. It brought you and it brought him as well.'

I hear a grunting sound. The second wheelchair is placed alongside mine.

'Say hello to our other guest Erma. Don't be rude.'

I'm heaving air.

'Say hello, Erma, or Harlan is going to hurt you again.'

I look. It's a man. He's not strapped to his chair but he isn't getting out of it on his own. I doubt he can walk. The man's head is freshly shaved and one of his eyes is bandaged shut. The lower part of his face is covered in jagged stitches. A thick piece of gauze holds his jaw in place and some sort of fluid is being pumped into him from a bag swinging from a thin steel pole mounted to his chair. As I'm taking all this in, the man's good eye twitches: a white dot amongst the purple bruising. He scans me with manic intensity.

The man grunts at me. The recognition hits.

Sam Hell.

The carpark. This man crawling away from me.

My hands dripping with blood.

'Erma!' screams Archibald. 'What did I just say! Be polite!'

I find my voice but it comes out quiet.

'Good, good mor—'

'Louder.'

'Good morning, Roberto.'

I see the door close and the world disappears into a void so rich and real that everything I've done in my life starts to play out in my mind. All the successes and failures that brought me here, they all jostle for attention in my subconscious like birds attacking me. This is Archibald Moder in my head. His advice scratching at me. For hours on end I see myself plotted out in a dark sky – for the first time in my life – and it's all one big pattern of flight. A map of four hundred sections. Clear. Emotionless. Except for some missing piece . . .

A line divides the map. A line between what's real in my past and the lies, the narratives, the delusions. My borrowed stories. My choices. That's all I am. I see that now.

Eventually, I sink.

Time evaporates.

A fever swells.

Ants find me in the hole and crawl under my scalp, creeping out of my ears and nose and from the ducts of my eyes.

I'm sweating, bringing something to the surface.

I'm close to finished.

SERO

43

You stand in the tall trees and hard rain and look into the mouth of the cave – the start of everything – and you know you need to go back inside.

The interior is as you remember.

Brown dirt.

Black ash.

Ochre blood on the walls.

You are only a short way in when the smooth stone pedestal appears. This is the pedestal from which you woke.

You climb up onto it and lie down.

You close your eyes.

The pedestal shudders and descends down into the earth below.

44

You drop smoothly through a corridor of rock into a colossal underground cavern the length and height of the forest above. It is a grim place. Sharp coal stalactites and grey rock. You look over the edge of the pedestal and see that it sits aloft a tall column that steadily draws you down towards a black lake.

A gentle mist soaks your skin until you crash through the water's surface wherein the pedestal continues to drop without you, leaving you suspended in the water, breathless and silent.

You search the void, hair swirling.

A long thin shape emerges from the darkness, moving like a snake. The shape is some distance away but as it draws near, you see it for what it is: a tentacle.

Another of these shapes appear.

Then another.

Then the whole beast comes into a view. A squid the size of a castle. An immense creature with mottled skin the colour and texture of manure and rotting fruit. Its tentacles swim past and the throbbing openings are like gaping mouths, opening and closing and trailing dark red ink.

Within seconds, the giant squid fills your vision, blocking the light from above. It envelops you. Its limbs close tight.

An eye peers out of the mess.

A mouth too. It gapes open, drawing water and shifting the current. As your body is sucked into the beast, you catch hold of one of its fangs, holding on. The water roars around you.

The creature emits a volcanic howl and shakes itself.

You lose your grip.

You disappear inside it.

45

Light sparks.

Red.

White.

Red.

White.

Red.

A room of red. A marbled floor. The walls and ceiling, bare. Bare and red, the red of innards and gore. Yet there is nothing organic about this room. There is a desk in one corner. The wall behind the desk glows, lighting the room, and you can see a woman sitting there, writing. She has long hair and wears a uniform of unfamiliar origin: the trousers of a man matched with a chest-covering that includes a druid's hood. Her face remains obscured by the light.

'What is this?' you say.

The woman startles. 'Holy shit.'

'Who are you?'

'Who am I?' she says. 'Who the fuck are you? How'd you get in here?'

'A squid took me.'

'A squid?'

'A giant squid. Where is this?'

'This is my home,' says the woman. 'It's where I live.'

'Are we inside the squid?'

'No. No, we're inside Erma now. That's the name of

251

this place.' The woman stands from her desk. She moves closer, studying you. You recognise her.

The girl from your visions.

The girl glimpsed in the dungeon.

She spots the change in you. 'Do you know me?'

'Dora.'

'That's right,' and she inspects you, her face close now. You flash back to Rohank screaming:

Go under.

Dora. Dora. Dora.

This is your heart, barbarian! Inherit your life!

Dora. Dora. Dora

She says, 'Who *are* you?'

'I'm Sero.'

'Never heard of you. But you look like something out of these books I read as a kid. Are you real?'

'Yes. Are *you* real?'

'Real enough,' she says. 'Do you have any idea why you're here? I've never had a guest before.'

'I've come for my memories. I'm without them.'

'Are you now?' she says. 'Hmmm, I'm not really in the business of gifting memories. That's not really my thing.'

'What are you? A mystic?'

'Near enough,' she says. 'Do you have gold on you?'

You nod.

'Well, then I can write you some memories, I guess. What do you want to be? A business executive? A public intellectual? A cage fighter? An amateur detective? Name your poison.'

'I want *real* memories. No more stories.'

The girl walks back to her desk. 'You don't scare me. You'll get what you're given. I think you should be a great hero. Violent but in aid of something noble and grandiose, someone likeable, relatable, friendly. Yes, that'll suit you well, I—'

Enough.

You draw your sword and stick Dora with the blade, pushing it through her shoulder. As the sword enters, a cold chill runs up your arm bringing with it a murky vision:

A house. A set of gardens. A pool. All of it familiar from previous visions. This is the land of summer nights. There are two figures in a pool, lit from a submerged orb.

One called Erma.

One called Euan.

They're apart but they're talking.

Both smiling.

You hover in the air above them, the pool a broad white rectangle. Slowly you slide down to them and in through the top of Erma's head, into her thoughts. You hear her and her voice says:

You ever meet someone and know they'll change your life? I have. That was Euan. Right from the fucking start.

The sensation didn't have a name but, looking at him, I knew he was going to shake things up and I was right.

Looking back, Euan presented choices. He was a fork in the road where there was only one path before. His arrival sheared my singular, young-person life into two new realms and led me so far down one of those paths that I forgot – for a long time – that another branch existed. I forgot that an intersection sat way, way back in the rear-view. A point of departure.

In fiction, these intersections are the 'inciting incidents' of a story. They're the situation that forces the protagonist into the plot. When executed in linear storytelling, the protagonist cannot return to how things were before the intersection, not once the inciting incident has happened. That incident is a portal. The writer pushes their character through it. The character is never supposed to have the agency to crawl back through, to go back up to the intersection and reconsider her options. To do this breaks the story and the story is the reality of fiction.

And so it is that Euan now swims across my mother's pool in a line that feels locked and unavoidable. A red thread joining us. There is no shifting him from this trajectory. No changing my response to it.

Not now.

He whispers, 'Marco?'

And I whisper 'Polo' and we both laugh as he slips his arms around me, pulling me into the kiss that opens up the other timeline.

46

'Jesus fucking Christ,' screams Dora. 'What did you do that for? Ahhh, fuck, *fuck*.' She grabs at the hole in her shoulder and writhes around in her chair, gasping. 'Am I going to die? Jesus.'

You tell her she'll live unless you stick her again. 'I want what I came for.'

'Yeah, yeah.'

'Now!'

'All right. Hold on.' She picks up her pen and starts scratching out words on a piece of parchment. As she writes, she mutters to herself. 'Oh, I guess. Yes, that'll do it. OK, OK.'

You feel a slight tingling sensation in your hand and open your palm. A clear canister materialises, some textile you do not recognise. When it's fully formed you hold it up to your face and say, 'What is this?'

Dora grits her teeth through the pain. 'I wrote you a potion. You drink that, it'll give you whatever you've got locked inside you.'

'I've had more than enough of these tricks,' you say, remembering the journey and its various hallucinations and elixirs.

'It's all I can offer.'

You bring the canister to your mouth. You take a sip. It tastes like water.

The woman watches. 'It's what you want, isn't it? It's your choice. Look, just fucking swallow it and get out of here.'

You turn away from her.

You stare into the red walls.

No.

You spit the potion out and swing the blade at Dora's neck, splashing her blood across the room in a gushing arc. As soon as the splatter hits the walls, it discolours the red there, stripping it away. As Dora gurgles in the background, clutching her throat, eyes wide, you inspect one particular splatter of blood on the wall. It glimmers like sunlight on water. You go in close and there in the blood is your reflection.

A mirror.

You look into it.

You recognise the face staring back.

ERMA

I'm gone, until someone asks me as much:

'Are you there?'

I think it's a hallucination. 'Fuck off.'

'Hey?'

'What?'

'The water is poison. You were right to stop drinking it.'

'Oh, OK.'

'You're detoxing. That's why you're sick.'

And there it is.

A pinprick in the wall of my cell.

The first dot of light.

The voice has a name. Laura. At least, she tells me that's her name. I can glimpse parts of her face through the small hole she's carved in the wall. Ginger hair, pale skin, glasses. She's one of the girls I saw in the corridor a few days or weeks ago. She visits me for ten seconds at a time.

'Erma?'

'Yeah?'

'You're not drinking the water, are you?'

A thin rubbery tube is pushed through the hole, blocking it momentarily. A muffled voice says, *Put this in your mouth.* I try it, some instinct kicking in. I sip on the tube and my mouth fills with cool liquid. I keep at it until I hear the sucking sound of the last drops being hoovered up from a plastic bottle.

'More tomorrow,' says Laura.

'Wait.'

'No. More tomorrow. They're coming.'

'Hey, Erma, are you awake?'

The tube comes through again and I drink. The tube disappears.

I ask her, 'How long have you been in here?'

'Two years.'

'Can you get out?'

'No. There's cameras.'

'Where?'

'I've gotta go. Don't drink the water.'

'Are you living out there?'

'Yes. There's a flat. I'm in the bathroom. I've got to go. They can see me in here.'

'Erma, drink this.'

'Thanks. How did you make this hole?'

'I used a butter knife.'

'Is that the only sharp thing you have out there?'

'It's all we're allowed.'

'Do you have more than one?'

'We have three.'

'Can you push one through?'

'Tomorrow.'

'Erma?'

'Where are the others?'

'They're scared. Here's the knife.'

I don't remember asking for this but I take it.

Laura says, 'You need to hide it or they'll hurt us if they find it in there with you. I mean it.'

'OK.'

'What are you going to do with it? Jimmy the lock?'

I say the first thing that comes into my head. 'I'm going to sharpen it.'

'Why?'

'I'm going to kill one of them.'

'OK. Be careful. If you can, kill the woman. The one in the dress. Her name is Sadie.'

'Is that his wife?'

'She pretends to be.'

'Erma, are you there?'

'I'm here.'

The tube comes through. I drink.

I ask the question I've been making myself sick over. 'How long have I been in here?'

'About a month.'

I do the maths, thinking about how much weight and power I've lost. 'I need more water. I need a supply.'

'I'll try.'

I sharpen the butter knife.

Three days later, they come for me and they almost catch me mid-workout. I'm partially rehydrated by then. Laura has taken her life into her hands and made extra trips to the hole. After some goading on my part, she installs a three litre plastic bottle of water on the other side of the wall, hiding it as best she can. I have no idea what's out there for her or how much immediate danger we're in but I don't need to know. I only have to elude detection for another week or two, another stretch of solitary darkness to get back into some kind of shape.

My cell is big enough. I can do a push-up in it.

I can do full squats.

Crunches.

I can run drills, lashing out at the darkness. I can work for hours.

Jab.

Cross.

Jab.

Kick low.

Jab.

Low cross.

Jab.

Kick.

And this is why I'm sweating when they open the door.

'She still looks sick,' says the thin woman in the black dress. Always the same dress. *Sadie*.

Harlan peers in. 'You sick, bitch?'

I've got the knife stashed in the corner by their feet. If they ever step inside, they will see it.

But not today.

Drew and a man I don't recognise drag me out of the hole and tighten the leather mask I have to wear when I'm going outside. Then they carry me upstairs in the wheelchair with Harlan meeting us halfway. They all want to stick around for my chat with Archibald – Harlan is worried: 'She looks fucking crazy' – but Archibald won't have it. He has me in the room where we first met. It's raining.

When we're alone, Archibald says, 'You look OK to me.'

I nod slowly, squinting around with veiled eyes.

'I take it you're drinking again,' he says. 'That's good, Erma. Good for you. You really had me worried after our last appointment.'

I nod again. I let my head flop around loosely on my shoulders.

Archie seems to buy it. 'Let's get started, shall we? Today's a big day. I've been studying your file and I'm happy to report that I've finalised your treatment plan. There's nothing too badly broken in you, nothing a little bit of flooding won't fix down the track. And Roberto's been telling Harlan he's keen to start helping out with that once he's on the mend. Drew as well.'

266

'I . . . I want to get better.'

I want to drive a knife into you, Archibald.

I want to live long enough to hurt you.

'Excellent,' he says. 'OK, let's start with some stories. I want you to tell me about your twin, this girl called Dora.'

'She's not my twin. I told you that.'

'Oh yes, that's right. She's younger, yes?'

'Eleven months.'

'And she's in Melbourne?'

'I don't know where she is.'

'You know your parents are worried about you, yes? They needn't be but they've been, well, visible.' Archibald puts a hand on a manila envelope that sits on the coffee table between us. 'We've had people out here looking for you, but we don't like to interrupt a guest's progress once they've started. Your mother, I must say, is an *interesting* woman. Very interesting.'

They're just words. He's just a man speaking. Stay calm.

'I believe your parents were notified of your disappearance not long after you came here. The woman who works with you, the troubled one, I know all about her, she's been raising hell down in the city. Your parents caught wind of it and came up from Melbourne. They aren't far away, Erma. Not far at all.'

'OK.'

Breathe.

'It's a funny story, actually. Your friend – what *is* her name? The Indian one – she's been causing trouble for years now. *Years*. Always going on and on about a couple of our guests. Our guests who, well, *they* don't want to leave and *we* don't want them to leave, so it's a load of bother. We've seen so much progress in Drew, in particular, since they came out here. If your Indian friend could see that, she might take a more constructive view of what we do out here. But no. That loudmouth keeps blabbering on, trying to ruin everything.' He pauses there. 'Is any of this registering? Am I making sense?'

'No. You lost me.'

He looks out the window and sighs. 'Your friend understood. The other one. Jenny. Lovely girl. An easy patient. Completely broken before she got here, of course. Addicted, thoroughly. But that helps sometimes. She had a sister too, didn't she? What ended up happening with Jenny, that was a mistake, plain and simple. It should never have happened.

'Sorry, I still don't . . .'

'You weren't supposed to be there that night, if you remember. If you cast your mind back, you were *supposed* to be in Spain. Poor Drew watched the flat for a week, trailing . . .' and he clicks his fingers.

'Kanika.'

'Yes, that's it. Kanika. She was house-sitting, wasn't she? Drew had her at your apartment every night right up until the night we sent Jenny in there for her. It was an exercise that would have really helped Jenny, I think. But it all went a bit pear-shaped.'

'Why would Jenny want to hurt Kanika?'

'Oh no. We told her she was going in there to shoot you. We just saw a convenient moment, so to speak. Jenny had all sorts of strange ideas about you. Those ideas really started to manifest during the early stages of her treatment. And shooting you, or a version of you – I mean, shooting Kanika believing it was you – it could have been such a win-win for her and us. And young Jenny really didn't need much coaxing. A bit of medication. A bit of therapy. Some time to reflect. She hated you already and when we threatened to bring her sister out here for a visit, that's about as much as it took to prepare her.'

'I saw Drew that night.'

'You did. And Harlan, in fact. They were both watching the sister, in case Jenny refused her treatment. I sometimes wonder what might have happened if either of them connected the dots and worked out who you were exactly. Harlan's not the brightest boy, unfortunately. But still, you weren't supposed to even be in the country, were you? No, poor Harlan had no idea. And yet he was quite smitten after seeing you that night. Quite smitten. Even more so after you fought off Jenny and he started looking into how you did that, your fighting and all that business.'

Archibald starts to turn newspaper clippings in the manila folder on the coffee table, eyes glancing down as he speaks. 'On the upside, this little mess brought you to us. So it wasn't a total waste of time. Except—' he sighs '—except for poor Jenny. But then that's the problem with dramatic interventions, they can be very unpredictable. I have no idea why she killed herself. Terrible. Just terrible. Now, oh dear, I feel like you've led me frightfully off-topic.'

Archibald gently taps his hand on the coffee table. He's thinking. He has his hand resting on a newspaper clipping, a quarter-page photo of my mother and father.

'Don't hurt them,' I say.

'Who? Your family? Never. Never! It's you, Erma, it's *you* who wants to hurt these two. I barely know them. *That's* what we were talking about, wasn't it? Yes, that's right, we were going to talk about your twin today. The magical Dora.'

'My sister.'

Archibald's eyes brighten and I see I've been played.

Stop talking.

This is a trap.

It's all been coming to this.

'No,' he says. 'There's quite a bit of biographical information in these news pieces and we did our own research as well.'

'And?'

Stop it.

Don't engage.

Fuck.

'Well that's the thing, isn't it?'

'What's the thing?'

'There's no sister. There's never been a sister. You are an only child, Erma. Always have been. On your own, your whole life. Dora is a figment of your imagination. As much of a fantasy as Sero. Dora's just a way of dealing with all the nasty secrets you've kept hidden, buried back there in your frail little mind. You need to be free of Dora, I think. It's definitely time.'

I can hear the wailing in my head before it belts out my mouth. The first scream almost chokes me and then all I'm doing is screaming. Not living, not breathing, not speaking, not thinking. Just screaming.

Back in my hole, I fall apart. My great unravelling.

It's starts with Euan.

Euan the handyman, the yardman.

Euan and I skinny-dipping at night in the family pool, a week into his employment, a week he spent reshaping the hedges in the rear garden as I read Archibald Moder novels on the deck. What happened in the pool wasn't such a big deal, not in and of itself. We were both young idiots, both fit and lean. Both up for it. Familiarity leads to attraction, as they say. And a week is familiar enough when you're that age.

But it kept going.

I got pregnant.

My mother paid for the abortion. I wouldn't tell her who the father was. I thought I loved Euan. Loved him enough to put my mother through that nightmare. She was raised Catholic, so paying for it made it even worse. In her eyes, she wasn't just committing a sin, she was spreading the corruption around, infecting me. That was one side of it. The other side was that – as a Catholic –

she knew someone she could call. She knew who to pay. She made the appointment from a number already in her phone, whoever that may have been.

Then I had the car accident – not Dora – on the way to the first meeting at the termination clinic.

I broke my arm and both my legs.

I completely wrecked myself. Just ruined.

I lost the baby.

The recovery was long.

Weeks.

Months.

My father was around for the first part but then he got back to work. He went back out there on the road, taking meetings in hotel lobbies and uptown bars.

My mother kept Euan around.

Euan dressed my wounds and helped me to the bathroom. He played the compassionate secret boyfriend but he also slipped into my room at night. I told him no but I couldn't fight him off in my condition. I couldn't move. Couldn't get away from him. Over the course of a long summer, I learned a lot about Euan. You never really know someone until they have power over you.

I survived it.

That's all that counts.

Eventually the visits with Euan tapered off and some-where in there, in the last days of that nightmare, I found myself smoking a joint in the upstairs en suite, spying my mother fucking Euan in the rear cottage down the yard.

I don't know how long it had been going on but I assume it was from the start. I figure that's why my mother employed him.

Two weeks later, my father comes home and we all sit down to dinner. Dad's so oblivious – or stupid – that he actually invites Euan to stick around and eat with us. Euan is, after all, the son of a family friend. And somewhere in there, in that family dinner after all we've been through together, in the white noise of friendly banter and *This is great, dear* and all the smiles and secrets and submerged horror, I snap and take a dinner fork and ram it into Euan's face repeatedly, creating wounds that require three dozen stitches and permanently blinding him in one eye.

I guess that's how I eventually told them what happened.

Not with words.

Not with treatment.

But with a kitchen fork and an out-of-court settlement.

After that, I headed north. North to where all communication with my past is virtual, at a distance, where nothing is real. I came north, to academia, where I studied narrative and built my own timeline with Dora.

Dora who wanted the baby, who still has the baby.

Dora who marries Euan instead of letting him destroy her family.

Dora who gives my parents what they want.

Dora who reverses and rewrites things so that none of us are hurt.

Dora the impossible.

My invisible sister.

The one who becomes the container for all the complicated things I just can't fucking live with anymore. The compartment. The version of me where everything worked out just fine and where all the violence inside me is totally unnecessary and unrequired and locked away. Inside me, Dora writes a version of the world where I don't have blood and viscera on my hands and where I can forget the appalling cries of my own mother, watching on as I try to kill her lover in front of her. The world where my father isn't holding my rapist, crying out for me to stop.

But not anymore.

Dora's done. Stripped away.

And here I am at last.

I know I'm near the end when Sadie starts talking to me more. 'Now, are you gonna behave? Because if you promise to behave, I might let you out to talk to the other girls for a spell. Might.'

She keeps the door open longer each time and I get a bead on her: drawn features, late-fifties, her skeleton body always draped in the same black tube dress hanging off her like an oversized sock. Sadie keeps a taser on her, giving it a buzz to ground home whatever she's saying.

'Now stay still while I put the mask on.'

Bzzzzzzzzzzz.

'Now heel for me, girl, that's right.'

Bzzzzzzzzzzz.

'Now promise me, go on.'

Bzzzzzzzzzzz.

I promise, every time.

The taser is a problem. I figure I've got one shot at getting out of here and the taser can stop me cold. On the other hand, when I've got the taser in *my* hand . . .

Sadie, I promise I'll behave appropriately.

I promise.

★

Then one night music floats down and heavy footfall moves across the ceiling. We have guests.

'Hey?' says Laura through the hole.

'What's happening up there?'

'Sounds like Harlan has friends over again. This might be it.'

'I'm ready.'

'We're going to be OK,' says Laura.

I say it back. 'We're going to be OK.'

I stand.

I start warming up.

An hour later, someone beats on the door of my cell and Sadie's voice says, 'Erma, do you want a shower?'

'Yes.'

The door opens and I'm already in position, already wearing my mask.

'That's good,' says Sadie.

Bzzzzzzzzzz, goes that taser. She holds it close and I can see blue flashes even with my eyes squeezed shut.

'Out.'

I step into the little hallway, careful to slump against the door frame as I move. I'm supposed to be bombed on whatever it is they're putting in the water.

She grabs my ear and yanks me up. 'Get on.'

On the way down the corridor, I try to slow her down – crying out in pain, dragging my shoulder against the wall – all so I can let my eyes adjust to the light. The corridor is less than a metre wide, meaning I can't throw a proper punch in here. Or use the walls. It's too tight.

The hall puts us out into a room lit with tube fluorescence. I make myself fall and scan around through the veil of my hair. It's the twenty by ten metre bunker I saw before: four bunk beds on one side and a kitchen on the other. There's a door ahead and another on the left. There's the grubby lino floor and three pairs of bare feet, ankles, shins.

The feet belong to the girls I'm trapped down here with. As Sadie yanks me back up, I get my first good look at them. They're all in their twenties. They look clean but emaciated and ghoulish from the treatments. Chalk-white skin. Ginger dye-jobs. Glasses. They all stare at me through the exact same set of lenses, each with the vacant eyes of the drug-addled and hopeless. Laura stands in the middle. She nods silently.

The door on my left opens.

A man steps out. He's big, tall enough that he needs to stoop to fit his frame under the bunker's low ceiling. 'Is Doctor Lecter joining us tonight?' he says to me with a smirk. I can't place his face but he doesn't look unfamiliar either. I suspect he's one of the orderlies who carries my wheelchair up the stairs.

'In there,' yells Sadie and she foists me towards the door. It's a bathroom. The bathroom Laura tells me adjoins my cell. It's a barren room with a tiled square in one corner for a shower, a toilet pedestal, a set of steel lockers and a small sink unit and cupboard. The orderly stares at me through the doorway as Sadie closes the door behind us.

'Strip' she says. 'You smell like shit.'

I slip my underwear down. It's all I have. That and the leather face mask. I touch the mask and look at Sadie.

'That stays on until you learn not to bite.'

'I won't.'

'I said no. Now don't just stand there looking at me like some retard,' screams Sadie. 'Get in that fucking shower.'

Bzzzzzzzzzzz, goes the taser.

Standing beneath the warm spray of the water feels jarring and alien.

'Wash your cunt,' says Sadie. 'Use soap.'

I turn away from her. I take deep breaths. The water trickles around the crevices of the mask. I start to get my bearings. I start doing the maths.

Two paces to the towel.

Five paces to the cupboard.

Seven paces to the door.

Fourteen paces, total.

A second per pace.

Three seconds to dry my hands.

Two seconds in the cupboard.

I turn off the water.

Sadie frowns. 'Well, well. You done already? Normally I have to drag you fucking girls out of here. Maybe you are gonna be one of the manageable ones?'

I tell her, 'I want to get this over with.'

'That's the spirit. I always tell the girls, you do as you're told and nothing bad will happen.'

Someone screams outside. One of the girls.

A heavy object hits the bathroom door.

Sadie jolts. 'What the hell?' She checks the taser, tsk-tsking. 'I told those girls a million times.' She puts her hand on the doorknob. 'Stay right fucking there.'

She goes out.

Adrenaline pumps through me. Time slows to a glacial set of precise movements.

I dry my hands.

I open the cupboard beneath the sink.

I grab the blade, the butter knife I've sharpened into a bright shiv. It lies on the floor of the cupboard, a few centimetres from the hole Laura made. Between scattered shampoo containers is the two-litre Coke bottle filled with water, the one that has kept me alive and clean these last few weeks.

I walk to the door, counting.

Seven.

Six.

Five.

More shouting from outside.

A girl yelps.

Four.

Three.

Two.

I step out.

Sadie is crouched down, coughing.

The orderly is also on the floor. Laura's under him, her arms flailing. He's beating her. I dart around them and go for Sadie, grabbing the left shoulder of her dress before she can get back up. She reaches for my wrist but I have the blade at her throat before she can do anything. I yank her up and around and back us both up against the wall and scream for everyone to stop moving.

The orderly sees us and lets Laura go.

The blade slices into Sadie's throat a little, a warm trickle at my fingers.

'Mum?' says the orderly, pleading.

'Stay the fuck down,' I scream back. 'Where's the taser? Laura. Find the taser.'

Laura scrambles around on the floor and freezes as she spots something across the room. One of the other girls steps straight towards me. She's got the taser in her hand, stretched out. She doesn't hand it to me. 'Mum,' she whispers.

I hear myself holler as the familiar blue crackle sparks but it's Sadie's body that convulses instead of mine.

Sadie slumps down.

There's a weird pause in the room.

I look at the girl with the taser and say, 'Don't do that again.'

'We've got to move,' says Laura. 'Time to move.'

Sadie blinks back into consciousness. I yank her up and shove her into the corridor. She says, 'Gary? Gary?'

I shout over my shoulder. 'Don't let him get up.'

The girl with the taser moves across the room. Sadie and I are about halfway along the corridor looking back when I hear the taser buzz again and the orderly in the kitchen cries out. Sadie screams back to him.

'Shut up or you die right now,' I shout.

At the end of the corridor there's a steel sliding door like something you'd see attached to an industrial walk-in freezer. There's no lock on the door, just a small keypad by the handle.

I push Sadie flush with the opposing wall. 'What's the passcode?'

'I'll do it,' Sadie croaks.

'No! Say it!'

She stops. There's a camera above the door, pointed right at us. All of this mayhem has probably taken about two minutes. Every second presents a threat. I take the knife and jab it into Sadie's side a few times. As she slides down the wall, I catch her under the chin and point the blade into her cheek.

I tell her, 'You're about to die right here.'

'One, two . . .'

She fucking pauses.

' . . . Zero . . .'

I let her go. Sadie actually smiles, some dark reserve left inside her.

I punch the code into the box.

One.

Two.

Zero.

Three.

I'm a researcher. I know Archibald Moder's birthday. *Twelfth of March.* The door slides open.

I step into a room. Timber veneer. Satin curtains. Warm lighting. My eyes skim over other details.

Steel hooks in the ceiling.

A bed with a harness and stirrups.

A video camera on a tripod.

There's a doorway in the far corner and a set of stairs leading up. I cross the room and have one foot on the first step when I hear something and turn.

Sadie has dragged her punctured body across the threshold of the bunker and is trying to escape. Our eyes lock for a split second – this elderly woman pleading silently – before her body is yanked back inside by one of the girls. Horrible sounds echo out of the corridor as I creep up the stairs.

There's a closed door at the top. A bright strip of light along the sill. I pat around for the knob and find it.

I hold my breath and twist.

The door opens.

The next room is bigger. There's a set of four green felt pool tables. No windows, suggesting we're still underground.

The door I've come through is a large book cupboard fitted to a hinge – a secret passage. I go to the nearest pool table. I put the shiv down and pick up a pool cue. Fighting with a staff isn't my style so I unscrew the cue and hold the two halves. This means I've got a weapon for each hand and far better reach.

I'm still weighing the pool cue batons in my hands when a man rises into view. He sits across the room on a black leather couch. He rubs at his eyes, having just woken from a nap. His eyes focus on me.

'Are you—' He smiles. 'Why are you naked?'

'I just stepped out of the shower.'

He gestures to my face. 'Why are you wearing *that*?'

The mask. I'm still wearing it.

I say, 'Who are you?'

'I'm Alfie. I'm one of Harlan's mates. Has the party started? How long have I been down here?'

I start to move towards him. 'How many people are upstairs?'

'I don't know. Why?'

'Alfie, there's four of us locked in the basement. They've been keeping us prisoner down there. You need to help us.'

'What?'

I see fear flush through his eyes. Animal instinct.

'What is this?' he says.

'Alfie . . .'

He makes a run for it. I catch him as he corners one

of the pool tables. My first few blows are sloppy but they work. He goes down. I keep beating him and he screams, 'OK, OK, OK,' but it's too late for Alfie.

When I'm breathless and finished, I notice Laura is by my side.

'Is he dead?' she says.

'I don't know.'

The other two girls appear. The one with the taser steps around Alfie's body, kneels down and stuns him on the side of his face.

'You should probably save the batteries on that thing,' says Laura. 'We might need it.'

The girl with the taser seems unnaturally calm. Still crouched by the body, she says, 'I remember this guy,' and gives the man another blast, this time burying the weapon deep in his crotch.

From the billiards room, we follow a polished concrete passage under the house. We pass a spiral staircase leading up and a series of locked doors. The music heard earlier grows louder and louder. The party is close now as we step into a dark open space.

I hit the lights.

Two black sports cars. A garage.

'Keys.'

We fan out and search the walls, benches and cupboards. We can't find them.

'We had a garage door like this,' says one of the girls,

the one who has remained silent until now. She points to a box mounted on the wall.

'Open it,' says Laura.

I hit the lights off again.

A motor whines. The giant two-bay door of the garage begins to rise. It's dark out but light beams in. The music comes louder still. We all duck under the door while it's opening and I feel the cool open air on my skin. There's a long paved ramp ahead, two ten-foot retaining walls either side, and a giant gleaming orb out of view on the ground above. We're about halfway up the ramp, running barefoot, when we hear the shouting.

Movement ahead.

One of the girls stops. Laura curses. She grabs my arm and pulls me back the way we came. I struggle for a split second but then I see it: a group of men walking casually over the lip of the drive above.

Voices echo around the hard surfaces.

'What are you girls doing out?' says a familiar voice.

Then we hear them laughing.

We run back through the garage and into the house, down through the basement corridor, past the locked doors and up the spiral staircase to the front door – the door I walked through of my own volition a few weeks ago – and at the door two men rush out of the darkness and grab Laura by the hair and arms. I swing with my two pieces of pool cue. I collect one of them around the head. The girl with the taser puts the other one down. Two more men launch in and one of these gets his hands on the taser and within seconds the fight becomes chaos. Impossible to track. They drag one girl to the ground, yelling at her, prising at her hands. Laura rips loose and both of us run to the second floor and we keep running. We need a window. We need a room with an open window. I don't know where the third girl is but more men come flailing in, shouting. There are five of them and they corner us. I land one good blow but someone gets the pool cue out of my hand and wraps it across my knees. I stagger around. I fight one of them as best I can. I punch him, knee him, drive his head into a protruding wall corner. After that, there's a scrum until I scrap my way loose, someone's wet hair in my hands,

288

slipping as I move. I run the length of the house, past the horrors of my fellow escapees under attack, past two more men coming up the stairwell, and into a cramped study in the furthest wing of the manse.

There's a lock on the door.

I have seconds to live.

I rip furniture around in an attempt to barricade the door but it's useless, just fucking useless, so I keep moving, trying to drag a dresser free from the wall. I'm crying and I can't stop. The tears start to blind me. I frantically tear at the mask without unbuckling it. The mask stays fixed but in the jostling around, I notice something rattling on the wall above the dresser.

I stare at it and the world falls away.

Is this it?

Is this where everything ends?

Is this the thing?

I hear men grunting and fighting outside but it's right at the back of my consciousness. I hear women's crying. Stomping. Cursing. Someone knocks on the door, testing the lock. Someone kicks at it but it holds. I keep staring at the thing on the wall above the dresser.

A voice says, 'Erma, come on out of there and we'll let you all live.'

It's Harlan.

I yell, 'Fuck you, I want to see Archibald.'

I reach up and pull the object from the wall.

It's a sword. A real sword.

A straight Dao in a sheath.

I draw it out and look at it. A single-edge blade. No hand guard. A worn grip. Old. But well kept. Recently sharpened too.

'Where's Archibald?'

I swing the weapon through the air, practicing my Thailand drills. The blade turns and glides. It's not too heavy.

'Erma?' Harlan says. 'What are you doing in there?'

There's something else on the dresser.

A mirror.

I look into it.

I take the mask from my face and it's you staring back at me.

YOU

The details of Dora's room fade and change and you find yourself standing naked with your sword drawn, waiting for the demons outside to make their start. They kick again at the timber door. Splinters spray. You move into position.

The last moment.

I of unlord, I of—

The door comes open.

A fiery explosion sounds.

A demon steps in and you catch a glance of some strange weapon in his hand as you swing through the entire arm.

'Harlan,' someone shouts.

The demon falls after his severed limb, wailing. You circle around and lunge for the next, a set of fluid movements now. You swing and the blade tears through more muscle and bone. The second demon drops, split, half decapitated.

Into the hallway beyond. You lose your footing, slipping in gore and dipping under the arc of a timber baton as it whistles through the air. You kneel forward and sweep the sword across the rotund gut of the thing with the bat.

His innards slop to the floor like muddied water from a bucket.

The rest of the demons turn and run.

You follow.

Ahead, in the strange hall, one of the demons squares up with you as the rest clamber around. It aims a long weapon. The end of the weapon explodes and some invisible arrow rips into your side. In return, you throw the sword through the demon's skull and his magic weapon slides across the floor, dropping over the edge of a balcony. You sprint to the fallen body and rip the sword loose and keep moving. The hallway opens to a stair beneath you and you watch as the remaining attackers rush and stumble down. One jumps to the floor below. As he lands a blast sounds, another thunder-crack. It's further away this time, coming from below. The side of the demon's head sheers loose. This panics the rest of the horde and they trip back up the stair towards you, hesitating halfway as they spot you standing at the summit.

A girl runs into view below, screaming. She is badly beaten, wearing a strange parchment-like robe caked in blood. In her hands, she holds the long weapon from moments ago.

The demons are trapped.

'Please,' cries one of them.

'We won't say anything,' says another. 'You can let us go. You can—'

CRACK.

The girl has fired the weapon again. The chest of one of the demons blasts open.

'Oh my god, oh, uhhh, shit.'

They run up the stairs. It is *you* they come to.

You with your full memory.

With history.

With clear purpose.

The hero.

You swing the sword.

Blood sprays.

A jaw is ripped loose.

A severed leg drops and tumbles.

A demon wearing a man's eyeglasses begs for mercy, holding his chest but standing tall and clear. You know the man: *glasses or no glasses*. He cries out as you swing the sword through his neck uncapping a sewer of gore inside him.

The girl with the magic weapon – *a gun* – collects another injured girl and calls out the name *Laura* three times.

A weak voice answers. Laura appears from behind a door on the second floor. 'I'm going to find a phone,' she says, limping past. 'Don't leave without me.' There is strange recognition in her eye. She knows your face.

While Laura looks for the phone, you busy yourself with the dying, staking each of them through the heart. None of them struggle. You find the one called Harlan back in the study where you started. Despite his missing arm, Harlan has crawled across the room, slumping himself against a wall, his skin as white as a statue. His eyes move when he notices you. He holds out a strange object. A small silver box. Some talisman that conjures occult recognition in you.

Dictaphone.

'Please,' he says.

You take the box and place it at his feet.

'Please,' he says a second time.

You nod. You cut his throat and let him die.

After Harlan, you check the rest of the upstairs chambers, looking for hidden creatures. You find an ailing demon with a shaved skull in one room. He hides beside a strange bed, his leg braced, a thin medical drip inserted into his arm. He stares at you with hate-filled eyes as you step closer.

'Bitch,' he mutters, barely able to speak. 'Bitch, bitch . . .'

You answer without thinking, in a voice you recognise.

'Hello again,' you say as you align the sword to the level of Roberto's eye.

You push it in slow.

There is one more. An old one, almost done for. He sits slumped into a couch beside a long wall of flat glass, just a black human shape against the dark landscape of trees outside. The man shakes his head in the darkness. 'Erma, what have you done?' he wheezes.

'I stopped them.'

'Oh Erma, you were doing so . . . Come, come and sit with me.'

You refuse. You stand in front of him, so close you can hear him panting.

'Archibald, I've got to go now.'

'Oh, I see. Leave me here, dear girl. There's nothing more I can do for you if you won't stay.' He waves you away. 'No more.'

You reach down and pull the old demon forward. You prise open one of his hands and put the sword in his grasp. You position it so his arm is outstretched with the blade pressed into his solar plexus.

'What are you doing?'

'I'm not doing anything, Archibald.'

'But, but what is this?'

You run the tip of your finger along the blunt side of the sword and say, 'This is a line.' You grab his hand and the shoulder of his nightgown and start to bring the two together, plunging the blade into him.

'Erma! Stop! *Stop!*'

'Fate is real, Archibald. You told me that.'

At first the blood drips out of him, a patter on the floor. Then it begins to spill quicker. He mouths your name. He tries again and gapes like a fish but no sound comes out – only blood.

'We're together now,' you say.

You push the blade harder and it sinks all the way through. He starts to squirm. 'Shhhh, Archibald. Listen.

Listen to it. This is the place where we intersect. It's happening.'

He's spluttering weakly now. Dying, you suppose. You tip him all the way forward until he flops to the ground. The stained sword comes out of his back and catches the light and you crouch down to check his pulse but some part of him is still in there. You rest a hand on the back of his head and pat gently. 'It's OK,' you say. 'I'm here, Archibald. I'm right here.'

The girls drape you in blankets and linens and together you leave the house full of corpses and walk the long road away. The road takes you down through gardens in the night wind. Tall pines sway in the shadows, roaring and dark until visited by other-worldly colours.

The blue of oceans.

The red of the desert sand.

A fast-changing combination sprays the leaves and branches as you collapse from fatigue, as if struck. Warmth spreads across your side. Sprawled out on the ground, you watch the night sky and feel yourself drawn towards the afterlife. The three girls crowd around you, shouting your name. You smile back at them and close your eyes. *At last.* You feel yourself fading. *At last.* The stone is cold beneath you.

PART FOUR

4 YEARS LATER
BRISBANE, QUEENSLAND

ERMA

The applause rings out over the auditorium, rising to a crescendo as the speaker readies her notes. She holds up a hand, motioning to the crowd for quiet. A ripple passes up the room as everyone sits down. The first words bellow out. 'Staff, alumni, guests and, of course, graduating class of two thousand and nine. I welcome you to the end of your journey. I'm sure the last couple of years have been trying, but here we are in this magnificent room together, celebrating your achievements, finishing the Herculean task you've undertaken. I'm here today to send you on your way. But before I do that, the Vice Chancellor has asked me to present you with a few parting words of advice.'

She's a famous writer apparently. That's what it says in the programme. I'm not sure what type of writer she is but the fawning parents around me all crane their necks to get a better look, so it's not literary fiction or peer-reviewed work.

'You see, a life such as mine is spent in glorious solitude. The life lessons I've learned are, for the most part, taught to me by people I've made up. Fictional characters. Things I've created. People and worlds and events under my strict control. In other words, I've spent the better part of my life talking to myself. I'm not sure I've got all the . . .'

Breathe.

I'm not good with crowds these days. After the escape and the trial, the throng of reporters and onlookers was intense and prolonged. It was too much attention accompanied by a barrage of opinion on something I barely understood myself. It was a bit much to take in.

Officially, I was accused of killing nine men. Unofficially, I was a hero. For a stretch, everyone wanted to praise me or spit on me. There were days of both. Weird, bipolar days.

Warrior, monster.

Innocent, murderer.

The whole thing wore at me, and when I wasn't in court, seeing the A2 colour blow-ups of the armless and disembowelled, the fury of all that jostling and probing and testifying was intercut with the *not-so-glorious* solitude of home detention and, later, a court-ordered respite in a clinic. Even then, no one could let it go. I got letters, apparently. Some of the men's rights groups picketed the clinic.

Onstage, the speaker laughs. 'I had to ask myself, was I a monster for seeing the structure of this terrible story, for noticing the beats of her misery, or was that my writer brain doing its thing?'

I've lost the thread of her argument.

'Couldn't it just be that the part of my psyche that's

professionally tapped in to how stories work silences the compassion and care momentarily? It's times like this I remember that writing doesn't inform and corrupt the human experience but, instead, mimics it, draws from it, tries its best to raise itself to the level of so-called ordinary life. Both distraction from and dedication to, that's what I do. And you all know this. How many times have *you* thought to yourself, *This is just like a movie*, but about your own lives? We all narrate ourselves. It doesn't matter who you are. We all seem to exploit the world, in aid of our stories.'

Breathe.

I got through it.

Of course, I got through it.

I survived the trial. There were *technicalities*. Lost evidence. Bungled paperwork. According to the lawyers, it might have been Archibald Moder who killed everyone, then himself. There was enough doubt. I think enough people wanted there to be.

After that, I got through the clinic too, probably because I needed it. On the whole, my recovery wasn't so bad after the initial commotion passed. The clinic was boring and tedious and emotionally difficult but I got to trust my therapists, especially the after-patient guy on the outside, Dr Dannen. At my very first session, Dr Dannen tells me to forget my mother. He gives me permission to do that, to admit that I hated her with good reason and to get on with my life. I took to it. In fact, within a few months of

Dr Dannen, I'm as done as I'll ever be with my family and my bad experiences growing up and *the time I got locked under the house by a group of men and maybe murdered some of them* — that's what Dr Dannen called it. Never a euphemism. There was no *incident* with him. Dr Dannen talked about it plainly because it wasn't really the thing that interested him. He was more interested in what I did next. He might have been the only one.

'And I say to you, class of two thousand and nine, seek out your story, seek out your passion, please seek it out.'

Fuck this bitch.

As famous as this author is, she's overstaying her welcome. The kid next to me is playing with his watch, flicking the light on and off. Beside him, an older man — grey beard, jeans, leather shoes — is staring at me, trying to place me. In a split second the recognition arrives and he looks away, turns his whole body from me.

Another round of applause rings out.

Aspirational music blasts from the PA.

The graduations start and we watch the students trundle up for their degrees. I hated these ceremonies when I was an academic. I'm here today because Laura from the house finished her thesis. I've only spoken to the girls from the house a handful of times over the years. Didn't want to intrude. Figure they must feel the same. But I wanted to see this.

When Laura's name is called, I stay in my seat but watch the overhead screen. She's virtually unrecognisable now:

long brown hair spilling out from under her mortar board. Actually, I'm not even sure it is the right Laura.

I check the programme.

It *is* her.

The whole thing makes me want to break down, but I don't.

I heard later that the university conducted their stupid sexual harassment hearing in my absence. Remember that? While I was locked in a dark hole under someone's house in the mountains, a couple of admin people from the university were at a meeting talking about my private life. Funnily enough, it didn't go their way. All the boys I slept with kept their mouths shut. Ryan Solis, the one Jenny was so enamoured of, went on the record saying we never fooled around while I was working on his thesis review, which is untrue – we did – and instead, Ryan talked a blue streak about Jenny and her quirks and contrivances. He told them how fixated she was on him and how unrequited it got. He told them about how *she* harassed *him*. And he told me all this over the course of a few afternoons in my apartment. He actually wasn't the only one of those guys to visit. Even Louis, my ex, called from the States to check in. All these men, all these smart young guys, curious all of a sudden. I guess most people don't know a murderer.

Sorry, *exonerated* murderer.

While I was a missing person, the university put me on unpaid leave and I segued from that to a disability package and then, a few years later, redundancy. It's fine. My parents bought my apartment outright – I couldn't stop them – so I have somewhere to live. And I have a new job. I have cash to live on. I'm keeping busy.

I teach private classes at the gym these days. If there's one thing a famous murder trial is good for, it's bolstering one's reputation as a badass. When I got out of the clinic and started back with Muay Thai, a guy approached me during a sparring session and asked if I'd teach his little sister how to break people's arms. He said it just like that.

A month later, I had five clients.

The month after, eleven.

All women. Girls, mostly. It's all I do now.

So here I am in the gym. Tonight, I've got a one-on-one with Barbara. 'Bangin' Barb', as the guys call her behind her back. An ex-model. Some kind of media consultant now. As far as I can tell, Barb has absolutely no reason to learn self-defence other than a sideways desire to punch people. I can come at that. She'll be in Muay Thai proper – or Brazilian jujitsu – by March. I can tell.

'Come on, Barb, you're too slow. Way too slow,' I shout.

The sweat pours off her.

I help her up. 'Get that fucking arm round, OK?'

Barb nods.

I try it again.

Barb brings the arm round.

Her eyes are scolding.

★

Two hours later, I step out of the gym air conditioning into a humid Brisbane storm and see a police car parked in the car park. Despite the downpour, the car door opens and an umbrella pops open above. A uniformed cop steps out. It's dark. She's close before I see her face.

Detective Edwina. I haven't seen her since the trial.

'Fancy a ride home?'

'This rain will pass. Might just wait it out.'

'Come on. I've got something for you.'

I look through the downpour. I can see the black outline of a person in the passenger seat. 'Who's that?'

'A friend. Come on. You're not in any trouble. Just take the bloody lift.'

I run to the car. When I'm inside, the passenger in front hits the interior light. She shuffles around in her seat. It's Kanika.

'OK, what the fuck?' I hear myself say, too flustered for much else.

'Kanika and I are old mates now,' says Edwina. 'What's it been? Two years?'

'Hi, Erma. How are things?' Kanika says.

'I'm OK. Not real into *this*. Whatever this is.'

'I tried calling,' Kanika says.

'I've been busy.'

'Sure,' she replies. 'I understand.'

Kanika never visited me in the clinic.

Never stopped by the apartment after the clinic.

'So, what's up?'

'Here,' says Edwina. She throws a plastic bag my way. Inside the bag are four plastic vials. 'That's a present.'

'Is it?'

'That's your DNA. I lifted those swabs from the rear car park of the Sam Hell nightclub a couple of years back. I was looking into the assault and disappearance of Roberto Agrioli. I believe you knew him. Reports were, you were snooping around the club. Anyway, that bag went missing during your trial and it really put a bit of a dint in the prosecutors' case. Got me busted back down to constable, too. But the thing is, I found it the other day. Seems it was at the back of my crisper the whole time. Figured you might like it as a souvenir or something.'

I turn the bag in my hands. The vials roll around. 'OK.'

'And we've got something else we want to give you,' says Kanika. She hands me a brown paper folder. Inside, there are photographs of a man. Young. Mid-twenties, brown hair, blue eyes, firm jaw.

'That's Simon Renner,' says Edwina. 'You don't know Simon. But you might remember his buddy, Drew Besnick. You . . .' She's almost says, *killed him*.

'I remember Drew.'

Edwina says, 'So this Simon guy, he disappeared after what happened. Fled the country. Finished his property economics degree abroad. He's a rich kid. In the investigation we turned up a bunch of possible suspects related to the Moder family. People like Simon who we know

307

visited the estate, frequent associates, people who deposited money in various accounts.'

'And people who had links to other girls from my research,' says Kanika. 'The uni stuff.'

'That's right,' says Edwina. 'We didn't find everyone.'

'And?'

'That's the thing. Mister Renner here is back in the country and he's a licensed real estate agent these days. He just oversaw the sale of an interesting property up on Mount Tamborine.'

'Let me guess. It's got a basement.'

'Correct,' says Edwina.

'Jesus. What are you going to do?'

'They're not going to do anything,' says Kanika. 'Nothing's changed.'

'Nope,' adds Edwina. 'No law against selling a house and not enough funding to look further into it.'

'Why are you telling me this?'

They look at each other.

Edwina shrugs. 'We're thinking we might pay Simon a visit. Or we're wondering, would you like to pay him a visit, with our help?'

I almost laugh.

This is insane.

'You want me to . . .'

They both look at me.

I put my hand on the door and pull the latch.

'I think I might walk.'

I'm half a block away from the gym when I calm down enough to stop running.

There's one part of branching narrative that doesn't work: the ending. There are things about it that don't add up. In Fighting Fantasy novels there's one conclusion and they almost all involve the promise of adoration and riches.

As the crowd cheers, the lizard king presents you with an ornate crystal box. Inside are 100 gold coins. You are insanely rich.

With the Choose Your Own Adventure books, there are multiple endings and some are coy and quick while others are more satisfying and meandering.

You finish the movie!

You have solved the mystery!

You explore the ship all the way home!

But none of this stuff takes any real stock of what *really happened*, which is that the protagonist got all their decisions made for them by a clear and present god, a god that – in the turn of a page – abandons them at the end of the story. If these books had proper endings, all of the characters would end up in clinics like I did, or in shanties in the mountains or wandering homeless. They would all be a wreck. Psychopathic. Insane. Delusional. At best, they might raise a cult of followers in your honour. *You*. The all-powerful thing that determined their decisions until you got bored. *You*. That monster watching death and destruction doled out as entertainment. What sort of god *are* you? The truth is, these characters would have been better off without you, don't you think?

Archibald Moder had it right. Last year I reread a few of his gamebooks as part of my treatment. His endings are completely distinct from the rest. There is always a fade-out in his stuff, a transition. Sero the Barbarian devolves into drink and stops listening to 'reason'. The Harner Princess finds another religion. The young boy of *Sky Traders* enters a type of hibernation, a self-induced coma where you can't get at him or his thoughts. True to form, at the end of his books, Archibald takes his characters back from the reader. He forces you – the reader – to relinquish your control. He reclaims his characters and, no doubt, imprisons them somewhere deep and dark in his fucked-up psyche. I'm sure he died with all those made-up people still bouncing around inside him. All those ghosts behind his eyes, haunting him relentlessly, and all those men around him riding along, building their own archives of horror and damage until I came along and put 'The End' in place. I hate to admit it but I know it's true: I did all of those dudes a favour. I was the one who finally healed them.

The rain thrashes down outside as I peel off my wet clothes and dump them in a pile on the bathroom floor. The bath is full of steaming water. I have a candle lit.

I step into the tub and draw the shower curtain across, placing myself in the little chamber. I close my eyes.

We're wondering if you'd like to pay him a visit.

That's what they said, wasn't it? I didn't dream it, did I? I get to wondering.

I can see parts of the story they're proposing in my mind's eye and not all of it makes me recoil in disgust. There's something there.

I could do it.

I could make it painless.

I could save Kanika and Edwina from the shit I see in my nightmares.

But I could also refuse, as well. I could keep myself the same. I could keep on living like I live now. I could keep this as the ending.

This.

But there are always options, I suppose. Options I need to decide for myself, that I can work through, a future without your prying, beady eyes, a new set of conjoined narratives that—

I blow the candle out.

Acknowledgements

I'd like to thank Tara Wynne, Angela Meyer, Liz Robinson-Griffith, James Buckley, Ben Willis, Benny Agius, Tegan Morrison, Ciara Corrigan, Andrew Nette, Liam José, David Honeybone, Lee Earle, DP, Bret, DT and all at Echo Publishing and Bonnier Zaffre. Special thanks to Clare, Woody and Ginger for their support and encouragement. I listened to records by Daniel Bjarnason, Ben Frost and Lawrence English during the writing of this novel.

**If you enjoyed *The Spiral*,
keep reading for an exclusive
short story from Iain Ryan . . .**

CLOVER

It rained on the bus from the airport and on the train from the bus terminal, and then it rained on Clover as she walked from the train to the house. Christa's assistant had been particular on the phone, specifying an exact time and route through the suburbs. The assistant made it clear that this visit was an imposition on *Ms Ellis* and that it needed to be done correctly, quickly, and on her terms, so Clover pushed through.

When she arrived, Clover spotted Christa in the window of her house. Christa stood there in a cream turtleneck, hunched slightly under the top of the window frame to see out.

Clover waved.

Christa backed away.

Clover expected the door to open but instead, an intercom box by the gate sounded. 'Who is that?'

'I'm Clover Mansfield. I'm here to interview you. I'm from the University of Nevada. I was told you were expecting me.'

There was a pause.

'You need to hold down the red button when you talk,' said the box.

Clover looked at the button. She held it down and repeated the introduction.

Another pause.

'I'm coming down,' Christa said.

The gate buzzed and Clover walked up the steps. There were herbs in pots by the door. Basil and mugwort in identical terracotta planters. Parsley sprang from a ceramic skull. At the sound of locks turning, Clover stood a little straighter.

'Good morning,' said Christa Ellis. Her gaze rested briefly on Clover then moved past her to the street. 'I'm sorry. I forgot about this. Please, come in.'

Christa took Clover's umbrella and coat and carried them to a rack. The front room of the house had a kitchenette and lounge area and two flat screen televisions mounted to a plain wall. Both screens played different programs with the sound turned down. The alternate flickering images were the only untidy parts of the room. Everything else sat in place: the coffee table square with the couches (magazines piled by width on top), and the couches equidistant from the wall and the small kitchen bench.

'Would you like a drink?' Christa asked.

'I could use a coffee, if you have a pot on. You have a beautiful house.'

'Thank you. How do you take it?'

'Black.'

Outside, the rain came harder, a wash of it colliding with the front windows, making the room feel bright and warm in the gloom.

'How long has it been raining?' said Clover.

'I don't know,' said Christa.

For the interview, they sat in her upstairs studio. Christa said the room had once been a formal dining area, but now an entire wall acted as a floor-to-ceiling screen. Two more television screens were mounted above an adjacent fireplace. Christa's computer connected to all three. 'The audio comes later in the process. I do that in there,' she said, pointing to an open doorway.

'Can I take photos?'

'I'd prefer to do it,' Christa said. She put her hand out for the camera then walked around the room with it. Christa checked each photo on the screen before taking another. To finish, she took a photo of Clover in her seat. She checked that photo too. 'Don't smile this time, just sit there.'

The camera chimed.

'You're very beautiful, you know. I guess you know. I didn't expect it. Most academics are…'

'Thank you.'

'Do you have a boyfriend?'

'No,' said Clover.

'Me neither. You can't imagine the people I meet doing this for a living,' said Christa. 'Do you like women?'

'No. Do you?'

'Not really.'

★

Images of gore and decomposition flashed across the wall. Christa spoke to them in a calm clear voice. 'I'm looking for how it makes me feel. The feeling is more interesting to me than how it looks. That's why I hate the term *visual artist*.' They were all films about empty rooms. In each one, something dead would appear.

A dead deer.

Dead dogs.

Corpses.

Each faded in, like a ghost. Christa said these pieces were about trying to capture attention and unsettle people quickly. It was old work. She disapproved of it now. 'The recent stuff is more honest to me, if that's a measure of anything.'

This later work was brutalist and dull. It drew on crime scene photography and photojournalism. Clover had read that Christa's father worked in a lab for the Boston police department. She asked after him.

'He was more influential on me as a person.'

The middle years of her catalogue proved the most interesting to Clover. She kept these questions to last and let herself feel a small glow of achievement when Christa became more animated discussing them. The Ellis middle period was maximal and grotesque. Filled with throbbing gothic reds and purples. Big fixed images of bruises, genitals and tongues. It seemed to search for beauty — formal beauty, like a still life — in the trash bag of human biology. And years later, Christa could still provide long, clear descriptions of it. 'It's transitional work and there's always a lot to talk about with transitional work,' she said. 'There's always a story. It's the easy stuff, in that way. The statement, the theme, it's right there. That's the only part of it that *is* easy, of course, but I'll take that trade-off any day of the week.'

After they finished, they went down to a kitchen at the back of the house and Christa made another pot of coffee. As the pot gurgled, they stood side by side and watched two silent televisions as they played some distance away on a blank wall. A news anchor beside a neon cartoon.

'I'm not sure if you saw it,' said Clover. 'But in the *New York Times*, Nicholas Faszo described your work as an "artistry of fear". Did you see that?'

'Do you think he's right?'

'I think he's close but, no. He's not exactly right. Nothing is ever exactly right, I guess.'

Christa put a teaspoon in one of the mugs, the steel clanging against porcelain in the quiet. 'I think he's right about me but wrong about everyone else. All art is about fear, isn't it? Life doesn't spare any of us. It's just a pedestrian thing to say about art.'

They looked again at the images on the televisions.

A crane demolishing a house and brightly coloured animals trailing animated stars and shapes.

Christa said, 'I think I work with panic, more than fear, anyhow.'

'I think you do too.'

'There's nothing like panic. It's a pure emotion.'

★

319

Clover planned to spend the night at a friend's apartment in the city, but as she left Christa's house the rain came down even harder, sweeping under her umbrella and across her glasses. It was so bad she retreated to the stoop of a pet store down the street. As she huddled there, her phone sounded. It was a blocked number.

'Hello?'

It was Christa, she could tell.

'Hello?' she said again.

'I think you should come back.'

'Okay,' she shouted as the wind came up, pushing rain out of a nearby tree onto the stoop.

At the house, she showered and put on a set of clothes Christa produced. Her assistant was a similar size, apparently. She also had a spare room and bed. Christa showed her the master bedroom before they turned in, and they stood together by the french doors and looked out at the city lights and the thunderstorm.

Christa said, 'I was standing here and I could tell it was only going to get worse.'

She was right. The weather raged all night. Clover stayed up. She didn't know what she was doing in the house, so she sat in her bed and worked on her laptop and when she did eventually sleep, it was only unknowingly and with her head resting against the headboard.

★

The next morning there was no mention of her leaving. They spent the day at Christa's worktable, silently working side by side. On an adjacent screen, two decaying corpses lay in vivid green grass. They were both fully clothed — 'Executed,' said Christa, 'quickly' — and filmed from the torso up. Christa moved the mouse over their faces, greying out skin and deforming them further. The images became translucent and overlapped. She pitched them together over a clinical white background until eventually they disappeared into a bright void.

In the afternoon, they shared cigarettes.

Clover made the coffee, for a change.

They ate dinner at a nearby restaurant.

'I'm not really into documentation, not like some,' Christa said over dumplings. 'I do it, we all have to do it, but this—' she waved her hand across the restaurant table, '—this is better. I want people to think about what I do. I just don't normally want to talk to people. Or steer the conversation. I don't want *more* artist statements. Most people who want to talk to me don't seem to understand that. I don't want more control. I hate control. I want less control.' That was the end of all discussion about what was taking place.

After dinner, they went to a neighbourhood gallery opening. No one approached Christa directly, they were always introduced. Clover could tell people were afraid of her. It wasn't how she looked, it was more the array of disconnects her image presented. Christa's life and work preceded her in every moment: the drugs and gossip, the rituals and orgies, the brutality, the line of disgruntled lovers. The bodies piled up. And yet none of this showed on the person who stood there in the gallery. There was a marked contrast. A disconcerting contrast, Clover thought. Christa's eyes may have been a little cold to look into, but otherwise she was another tall, stately woman in a room full of them.

There was an after-party and a back room. People huddled and shouted. They crowded around artists and rocked on their heels, half listening, chewing their jaws. Clover knew the crowd well. A man with cropped hair and a ring on his thumb came close to her ear and said, 'Let's get out of here.'

'No, I'm okay.'

Christa stood nearby. Clover could feel her eyes on her.

'At least let me buy you a drink,' said the man.

'No one's buying drinks in here.'

'Well, maybe—'

'You done?'

He walked away. Christa circled back. 'Come with me,' and she took her hand. They found a bathroom stall and Christa handed over a bag of powder. Clover tapped out two lines on the bench above the pedestal, took a five dollar note from her handbag, and snorted it back. She said, 'Don't look at me. I always sneeze when I take this stuff.'

Christa had her turn.

After a long moment, Clover breathed out. 'I was wondering if you still partied.'

'People like me never stop altogether,' she said.

'Don't need to?'

'Need, want, can't, won't. It's all the same after a few years.'

Back at the house, they sat in the lounge and talked down the jitters. At the end, Christa made her move as Clover expected. She let the artist kiss her before gently touching Christa's face and apologising.

In the morning, Christa sat at the table working. 'Hello again,' she said.

They ate.

Clover checked her email.

She took a shower. While she stood in the bathroom flossing, Christa knocked at the door.

'It's okay,' said Clover.

The door opened a few inches. Christa had a phone in her hand. 'Can you drive a car?'

'I can drive an auto. Why?'

'How would you like to come for a ride with me?'

'Where to?'

'The country. It'll be good for your piece, I promise.'

Clover turned back to the mirror. 'Sure.'

Christa closed the door.

Outside, a man in a suit stood on the sidewalk beside a dark SUV. 'Jeremy, it's nice to see you again,' said Christa as she came down the stairs. She carried a long, black bag.

'Always a pleasure, Ms Ellis. I've been told you're driving yourself today?'

'Yes,' she said, but Clover drove. Christa directed her south out of the city. Within the first hour, it began to snow and by the time they reached Champaign, the roads were slick with ice banked up to the gutters.

'It's going to be a cold winter,' said Christa. Her phone chimed. She checked it.

They drove all morning. Christa had Clover turn off the interstate and drive further into the flat country. They came to a small township, a stark place with low-set houses spread apart and all of them back from the road. The town centre had an old stone library, a police station, a gas station, a few stores and not much else. They passed a snow-covered sports field — or a racetrack, it was hard to tell — and beyond the snowfield stood a menacing grey water tower, its bulb-like head propped up on four thin steel legs. 'That's it,' said Christa.

They parked at the base of the tower. Christa removed her bag from the trunk and stepped across to one of the tower's legs. A metal ladder ran up the leg to a rickety-looking platform running the perimeter of the basin. 'I'm going up,' she said, slipping on a pair of gloves.

Clover took it in. The tower looked about a hundred feet off the ground. 'Really?' she said.

'We'll be fine. Do you not like heights?'

'No,' said Clover, a lie. 'I'm more scared of falling. Aren't you scared of falling?'

'We won't be up there long. You don't have to come but I think you should.'

Christa slung the black bag over her shoulder.

She started climbing.

Clover took hold of the ladder and followed. The rungs were dry in the centre and rusted so they gripped to her gloves and shoes but when she was a few feet from the ground, Clover ran her hand along the painted sides of the ladder, and they were like glass. As she went further up, she concentrated on her legs and hands, slowly finding a secure footing for each step before taking another. She was slow.

Up on the platform, Clover took in the view and the emptiness of it. The black car below, a dot. The narrow stilts holding them in place. The tiny township. The houses and trees huddled together in a white expanse, the roads criss-crossing the snow like ribbons. The sun sat low in the sky now, dim behind grey cloud. Clover willed herself to move, to walk along the platform. She moved around and looked at the tank with its rusted seams and weathered paint. On the other side, she found Christa hunched over a demountable tripod, adjusting the lens on a camera. Christa pointed into the distance where a group of people stood in a snowfield. The area was cordoned off with tape. There was a van and car off to one side. A flickering light.

Christa's camera clicked and whirled. 'Look,' she said, motioning to the telephoto lens. 'The police just got here.'

Clover placed her eye over the camera's viewfinder. A

tall bearded man and a middle-aged woman, both dressed in long dark coats, stood in the snow. Off to one side was a plump looking policewoman, hat in hand, with her partner. There was a photographer as well. They all stood around something in the snow. When it came into view, Clover moved back from the viewfinder.

'Look again,' said Christa.

Clover looked. Two young boys lay in the snow. They both had head injuries. Blood haloes in the surrounding white. They looked like mannequins.

'It's not how you'd think, is it?' said Christa.

'How do you mean?'

Christa moved back behind the camera and started snapping off photographs. 'It's not like *my* work,' she said. 'Something like this is . . . it's always so still. There's that total absence of movement. You can only see it here. You can't recreate it. Trust me, I've tried. And this guy . . . this guy is nothing if not consistent. He always dumps them in the snow. Always clean. I'm starting to think he's some sort of minimalist.'

'What are you talking about?'

The police car reversed out from the crime scene and onto the road. It came back towards town. Clover watched the car snake through the streets and around the sports field.

'They're coming to tell us to get down,' said Christa.

The camera whirred.

The police car stopped below. A car door slammed.

A voice called up.

'You go,' said Christa. 'Tell them we were up here taking stills for a book about Illinois, when we saw the bodies. Or something like that. She won't give you any trouble.'

Clover didn't move.

Christa turned to her. 'Don't tell them who I am, or we'll be here all day.'

Clover walked around the tank to the platform opening.

On the ground, the policewoman called up again. 'Be careful now, Miss. You can slip and break your neck up there.'

Clover sat down. She gave the policewoman below a short wave before rubbing her hands together and reaching for the ladder. As she started down and her head dipped below the platform, Clover felt light-headed. She took another few steps lower and stopped.

She waited.

Fighting back all her instincts, she looked down past her feet to the ground below. As she did, her hand knocked a splinter of ice free and it fell, giving the height perspective. This wasn't right. She heard footsteps on the platform above. The whine of a telephoto lens directed at her. Clover hugged herself to the ladder and perched there, suspended in the cold wind far above the ground, everything real and dangerous suddenly, but also rich and deep. It terrified her. It felt like new information, like living and dying at the same time.